"Your postcards from the cruise ship always make Belle smile. She saved all of them."

April flushed. How could she confess that sending those cards kept her connected to the little girl she had helped care for and the man she had been in love with? She had met other men on the cruises, but no one had ever been able to match up to Matt Carpenter. Or maybe no one had been able to match up to the romantic fantasy in her head of what Matt and she could have been if everything had been different.

She should let go of it. She had been awarded her big promotion now. When she was done here, she'd get her uniform, her very first uniform. With a single stripe, but she'd make it two as soon as she could. That was where her future lay.

Her infatuation with Matt had to end. She needed to see him for what he truly was. Just a man. Not someone special.

Certainly not The One.

Dear Reader,

Have you ever made a New Year's resolution? I think all of us have at some point in our lives. And we all know how hard it is to stick to it. So I hope you can identify with my heroine, April. She is facing a serious dilemma as the New Year begins. She has finally been promoted to officer on the cruise ship where she works, but to embrace this fully, she has to cut some emotional ties with Heartmont, the small town where she grew up.

But how can she when there is still that tug on her heartstrings whenever she sees Matt Carpenter? Matt never seemed to reciprocate those feelings, though. Isn't it silly to hang on to a feeling that can never have a future? Should she not finally move on? So that is what she resolves to do for New Year's.

April has always achieved what she wants. Will she also succeed this time? Or could it even be better for her not to?

I hope her story of finding love brings a smile to your face and that you enjoy your time in this community where people tend to each other and love triumphs against all odds.

Warmest wishes,

Viv

HEARTWARMING

The Rancher Resolution

—

Viv Royce

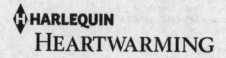

ISBN-13: 978-1-335-47566-4

The Rancher Resolution

Copyright © 2024 by Viv Royce

Recycling programs for this product may not exist in your area.

For questions and comments about the quality of this book, please contact us at CustomerService@Harlequin.com.

Harlequin Enterprises ULC
22 Adelaide St. West, 41st Floor
Toronto, Ontario M5H 4E3, Canada
www.Harlequin.com

Printed in U.S.A.

Viv Royce writes uplifting feel-good stories set in tight-knit communities where people fend for each other and love saves the day. If she can fit in lots of delicious food and cute pets, all the better. When she's not plotting the next scene, she can be found crafting, playing board games and trying new ice cream.

Books by Viv Royce

Harlequin Heartwarming

Heroes of the Rockies
Winning Over the Rancher

Acknowledgments

A heartfelt thanks to all authors (especially Harlequin authors), editors and agents who share online about the writing and publishing process. Special mention goes to my amazing agent, Jill Marsal, and my wonderful editors, Adrienne Macintosh and Natalia Castano, whose feedback is always spot-on. Thanks also to the rest of the dedicated team at Harlequin Heartwarming, especially the cover design team for the evocative cover.

CHAPTER ONE

AIRPORTS WERE A great place to people watch. To sit and observe how nervous elderly couples kept asking each other if they really had their passports and boarding passes, how mothers calmed excited kids and how business executives tried to finish all-important emails amidst the noise the others created.

It always made April Williams smile. She had traveled so often, all over the world, that airports almost felt like home to her. She was familiar with all the sounds and smells, and she didn't get upset anymore about sudden delays or the prospect of her luggage ending up in a completely different destination than she did. She was calm whatever happened, a skill also acquired during her work as cruise attendant.

Still some sort of nervousness crept through her system right now as she stood waiting for her luggage to appear. Nerves that only assaulted her at this particular airport. Because she was going home to Heartmont, that small Colorado town at the foot of the Rockies where her family ran a ranch with livestock and apple orchards. That town she had grown up in thinking she'd stay there all her life. But she had left, quite abruptly, because she had seen no other way. And whenever she went home, on leave, bittersweet memories surfaced and she felt the pain again of the decision to leave and everything that had brought her to that point. All the reasons.

"Hey, little Miss Sunshine." The warm male voice came from behind.

April froze. That was one of those reasons.

She turned slowly, pasting on the smile she always used with unhappy passengers. She could be cool about this, strictly professional. It didn't matter at all that the man who stood behind her had broken her heart nine years ago.

In his midthirties, Matt Carpenter was as tall and broad shouldered as he had been in high school where he had easily made the football team. He wore a leather jacket over a checkered shirt and stone-washed jeans. He still had his dark curls and those irresistible chocolate brown eyes that sparkled as he looked at her. Her breath caught for a moment as he stood there before her, materialized out of nowhere and giving her that wonderful warm smile. But she had long since learned it wasn't a special smile for her. Matt was friendly to everyone. And he liked to tease her in particular. Little Miss Sunshine, the nickname from the time she had taken care of his daughter Belle after his wife had died unexpectedly.

Everything in Matt's life had happened on an accelerated time line: he had married the love of his life at eighteen, and at twenty-three, after a tragic plane crash had swept his wife away, he had suddenly found himself a widower, a single father and the proprietor of the ranch-style hotel his wife and he had taken over from Matt's parents.

At a time where others might graduate college and look for a first job, get engaged or still be dating, Matt had faced a crying little girl asking for her mommy and the responsibilities of a business that had to provide steady income. Matt's father, who lived with the young family, had been a big help, but more hands were needed and April, who had been fresh out of community college with an associate's degree, had been looking for a local job. Bonding quickly with lovely four-year-old Belle and spending lots of time with Matt as well, she had fallen hopelessly in love with him and he hadn't had a clue. She had believed they were growing closer especially as he had helped her through a dark time in her life after her father's sudden death and then suddenly everything had been broken and she had left Heartmont. Had left her dreams of ever loving Matt and being loved in return. And still as she faced him now, her heart made a silly leap inside her and her knees grew weak.

What was he doing here? Why did he have to be here, of all people, when she arrived home? She had hoped to avoid him, or better even to see him from a distance and discover she wasn't feeling anything anymore. That her infatuation of old had disappeared and she could look back on it

with a smile but without being emotion-
ally invested.

The breathtaking turmoil inside her told
her it wasn't meant to be.

"Where are your bags?" Matt asked.
He still had that wonderful warm baritone
voice that made a shiver go down her spine.

"My bags?" she repeated, unable to tear
her gaze away from the light shadow of
stubble on his jaw.

"Yes, I assume you didn't get here with
just the clothes you're wearing. Don't women
need a ton of everything? Belle keeps telling
me I have no idea how that is."

The mention of his daughter made April
smile. She had babysat Belle often, cooked
meals for her and even done a few outings
with both the little girl and Matt. Feeling
part of that little family had meant so much
to her. Even when she had left town, heartbroken, she hadn't been able to tear herself away completely. She had kept sending
Belle postcards from all the exotic destinations where the ships she worked on
docked and Belle had sent letters and later
emails in return. Their connection might
be more casual because April no longer

lived in Heartmont but still she had a fond feeling whenever the girl's name came up.

Matt's smile deepened, pushing a dimple into his left cheek. "Your bags?" he pressed.

"I'll get them." April turned away with a flush. Fortunately, at this small airport the luggage pickup wasn't far and her single suitcase had just appeared. She liked to travel light. Hoping Matt would ascribe her high color to exertion or the heat in the reception hall, she grabbed the bag. It felt like a desperate reach for something solid that would keep her from getting totally knocked off her feet again by this man.

"Let me carry that," Matt said and gently pulled the suitcase from her. His fingers brushed hers and a warm feeling seeped through her hand into her arm. It spread like ink soaked into tissue paper and settled in her heart. Something so familiar and feel-good, and still so unwanted. She shouldn't be feeling this. She didn't want to see him or talk to him. Everything he said would make the connection stronger, revive the old bond.

"Why are you here?" she asked. She couldn't keep a sharp edge out of her voice.

"To pick you up." He eyed her innocently.

"You knew I was coming? How?" She hadn't told Belle in her last email, because she had been worried the girl would invite her over to the ranch hotel and she didn't want to go there. Once she was back in town, she'd set up a meeting with Belle on neutral ground.

Matt explained, "I was at the orchard this morning and your mother told me." The orchard was Williams Apple Orchard, located a few miles outside of Heartmont, and part of the ranch her brother, Cade, ran ever since their father had died of a heart attack ten years ago. Dad's death was so unexpected that April had been completely disoriented. She had walked about in a daze, not knowing how to make sense of all the emotions washing through her. Losing her beloved father had been hard but on top of that, she had to deal with Cade who had started to act as if he was suddenly entitled to make all the decisions at the ranch… He was a good guy and she did love him, but he could be so stubborn about doing things his way. He didn't ask for advice, didn't seem to need help. She had felt locked out, even superfluous. Her ideas didn't seem to matter because Cade could do it all by himself. That had also contributed to her decision to leave. Maybe she had hoped that Cade would miss her and ask her to come back?

He hadn't so apparently everything had gone fine without her.

Matt continued, "Your mother was a bit worried about who could pick you up as Cade was busy with his girlfriend for the celebrations tonight."

Yes, since the summer, Cade actually had a girlfriend. April hadn't met her yet but she had heard a lot about her. Especially the phrase, "Lily changed everything around." For Cade, for the ranch after a storm had hit, even for the town with all of her brilliant marketing ideas. April was happy for her brother, Ma, the locals, but it did make her feel even more superfluous. As if there was no place for her in Heartmont anymore. Maybe that shouldn't hurt, as she had her own life, her career and a shining future ahead of her, but still… Whenever she traveled home, something tugged at her heartstrings and a voice in the back of her head asked her if she was really happy living as she did. Far away from the country life that had once fitted her like a glove.

"What celebrations?" she asked quickly to divert her thoughts.

"The big New Year's Eve celebrations in town." Matt made a dismissive gesture as if he didn't much care for them. "There will be food and music, dancing, fireworks. It's been advertised for weeks. I've referred all the hotel guests to it and will be attending myself, with Belle."

They were walking side by side out of the airport reception hall into the parking lot. The wind hit her cheeks like an icy breath on her skin and the scent of snow was in the air. April looked up. "If it isn't clear tonight, it's going to be a problem for the fireworks." Her mind was already reaching for a solution, but she realized that wasn't necessary here. She wasn't working. They could very well manage without her impromptu advice. After all, nothing was more annoying than people butting in when no one asked them to.

Matt hmmm-ed. He pointed ahead to

a dark red SUV that was parked beside a yellow compact. "There's my car." The sturdy SUV had a symbol of a running horse on the side and white lettering: Carpenter Hotel Ranch—Western Experience. Established inside a former ranch house and stables, the hotel had a Western theme in the rooms and offered guests the opportunity to explore the area on horseback or, if they weren't experienced riders, in a horsedrawn cart.

At the thought of horses April's stomach clenched. She knew she hadn't been to blame for the accident with Flame, but her decision to go against Matt's explicit instructions about that particular horse had caused the breach with Matt that had sent her away from Heartmont. He hadn't accepted her apologies, but simply agreed with Cade's assessment it was better if she stopped working at the hotel. Like he had decided that, after one mistake, he couldn't trust her anymore.

After all they had been through together, he had simply let her go. He had said he was sorry and it was better this way, but she had never truly understood why.

That was a long time ago, but still… As they walked here together, it grated that he hadn't said outright that he was angry with her. That he thought it had been irresponsible and that he was disappointed because he had believed he could count on her to follow instructions and not endanger the horses or herself. It would have been hard to hear him put his feelings into words, but he had every right to say it. If he had only been honest with her. Not hidden behind a wall of silence.

Matt put the suitcase in the back of the SUV and then opened the passenger door for April. "It's probably chilly inside as well, but I'll get the heating on in a second."

The car smelled of Matt. He had this particular vanilla aftershave he had used for as long as she could remember and the scent wrapped itself around her as she settled in the seat and clicked the safety belt in place. She so wished he had switched to another aftershave, that he had changed his looks, that he had suddenly become a stranger whom she didn't recognize anymore. A man who talked too much and only about himself, someone who was easy to dislike.

Why oh why did he have to be nice, considerate, handsome, so much like the Matt she used to know?

It was really unfortunate he had come to meet her. She was tired from the long flight from Miami, emotional about coming home and then to find him waiting for her. It was a recipe for disaster.

Nonsense, she chided herself, *he wasn't even waiting for you in any personal sense. He merely obliged when Ma asked him to fetch you. He couldn't say no to her, even though it was inconvenient. It's that community thing where you step in when someone asks you to. It's probably just another chore to him.*

She had to imagine that he hadn't wanted it, had been talked into it, that he was sorry already. That way she could keep the memories at arm's length. And the longing for those old times when they had understood each other and she had felt so safe with him.

Matt slipped in beside her and turned the ignition on. He rubbed his hands a moment. "I hope you don't mind."

"Mind what?" she asked in confusion.

"That *I* came to get you."

The emphasis puzzled her. She assumed Matt had never noticed her feelings for him and believed that they had parted on good terms. Yes, he had fired her after the accident with Flame, but that had been done at the request of her brother. She had always assumed Matt believed he was doing what her family wanted, what was best in the situation. Why would he think there were still ill feelings on her part after nine years? Most people forgot much sooner than that.

Avoiding looking him in the eye, she said, in a forced cheerful tone, "Not at all. As long as I can get a ride home, I don't mind at all who is driving." She loosened her scarf and Matt focused on the traffic in the busy parking lot. Even though it was a small airport, there was lively activity on the last day of the year.

"Lots of people coming home for New Year," he observed. "I suppose lots of people will also be cruising?"

"Yes, certainly. Christmas was incredibly busy and New Year is the same." April folded the scarf into fours in her lap. "People love the glam on board with the champagne dinner at night and the dancing… Counting down to twelve o'clock together." There was something special about celebrating New Year's Eve on a cruise ship. She had done it numerous times now and still the atmosphere got to her every time. She could readily imagine how it was for those experiencing it for the very first time.

"If it's that busy, I'm surprised you could get a leave," he observed.

"There are hundreds of employees aboard those huge ships. Everybody has their allotted task, from ensuring the buffets are properly stocked to keeping the deck areas tidy or working in one of the shops, bars or the casino. Besides, I haven't had a vacation in quite a while. The higher you climb in the ranks, the less free time you have." She wondered if this was a good moment to bring up her big promotion news, but it might sound a bit braggy, coming out of the blue. And her closest family didn't even know yet. She should tell them before she shared with others.

She continued, "Ma gave me a hard time that she wanted me to come home. She kept repeating the fact I haven't even seen my new nephew yet. Gina's little boy is almost three months now and I have yet to meet him."

"Don't you like coming home?" Matt's voice was brisk as if it was a normal conversational question. But for April it was connected with so many feelings. Her guilt and regret about the situation with Flame, her grief and loss after she had to leave her job at the hotel and the little family she had become so attached to. Feelings she didn't want to have right now as she sat beside this man who had played such a big role in her decision to leave nine years ago. But she was no longer twenty-one and aching for Matt's recognition that he needed her, or Cade's admission that he wanted her input about the ranch. She had built a beautiful career in the travel industry and recently received a major promotion. It was time to leave the past behind her and accept that maybe the word *home* carried a different feeling than it had when she had been younger but that was a normal consequence of growing up and finding her own place in life.

She tried to sound casual as she scrambled to list a few innocent reasons for her hesitance to return to the Williams ranch. "It'll be pretty crowded at the ranch, you know. Cade's girlfriend is staying and Gina is settled there with the kids."

"But you love children, right? You were so good with Belle when she was little."

Yeah, that's why you let me go. April turned her head away to look out the side window. "Of course I love children. But the twins seem to be in love with Cade's girlfriend so they won't really be waiting for me to drop by. It's Auntie Lily this and Auntie Lily that if Ma is to be believed." April realized she was clenching her hands and relaxed them. She didn't want Matt to think she resented Lily's popularity. It wasn't about Lily really but about the unsettling feeling there wasn't a place for her in Heartmont anymore. People had moved on, lives had developed in different directions and… She was the outsider, just breezing in for a few days. Not someone who belonged here. Even Lily who had come from the big city to help with marketing the ranch was more a part of the family than April was.

At least, that was how it felt. But she had to get over that silly feeling. She rushed to explain, "I just have to get used to it, you know. My brother with a woman by his side… I'm really happy though that Cade found someone. He was alone for too long."

She took a deep breath and steeled herself mentally against the answer before asking, "How about you?"

"Hmmm?" Matt asked as if he didn't follow.

"How have you been?" *Coward*, she chided herself, *you should have asked, "Are you still single?"*

But why would I care?

She did cast a quick look at his hands on the wheel. No wedding band in sight. Of course not. Belle would have told her if her dad had remarried. Still, would she mention it if he was dating? Probably not. Their emails were infrequent, especially in the last few months.

"Okay, I guess." Matt shrugged. "Busy with the hotel and the horses. Trying to raise my daughter single-handed. Of course there's Dad but… Well, Belle is at an age now where she doesn't share much."

April nodded. It would probably have been easier if Matt's mother had still been alive and could have talked to her granddaughter. But she had passed away even before Belle was born. And after Matt's wife had passed away as well, it had been just two men and a four-year-old girl, trying to make do. She was sure both Matt and his dad had showered Belle with love, but as she grew up, she had to want a female influence in her life, someone to talk to and confide in. April's last two postcards had gone without a reply. She had accepted with a little sigh of regret that Belle was probably too old now to appreciate them. "Sixteen, right?" she asked to keep him talking.

"Right. She's doing great in school and she volunteers at the library. She thinks up projects there to get kids reading and… But you probably know all about that already from her emails."

April nodded. She had always been glad Matt supported her wish to stay in touch with Belle, but right now she wondered if it would've been smarter to break off all contact and avoid the ongoing reminder of the dream of a family she had lost.

"I'm really proud of her," Matt said.

"But…?" April queried. She studied Matt's features closer. A sort of frown sat between his eyes.

"Is there a *but*?" Matt asked.

"There usually is." April settled better in the seat and patted the scarf in her lap. "It can't be easy to raise a child on your own, and especially a girl. I mean… You're not exactly a big talker and…"

"Oh great, so it's my fault that whenever I ask her about friends or something, I get the cold shoulder?"

April grinned to herself. "Friends as in boys, I presume?"

Matt had the decency to turn red under the collar. "I'm generally interested in the people she hangs out with…" he protested weakly.

April snorted. "You do mean boys and Belle knows that. She won't let herself be quizzed only to then get a lecture from you."

Matt glanced at her. The look in his deep

brown eyes was genuinely worried. "Does it make me such a bad dad if I want to know who my daughter is seeing?"

"No. It's logical. But I know it doesn't work." She hesitated a moment and then added, "I know from experience. I didn't have one father growing up, I had two. Big brother Cade was always watching out for me, you know, making sure I didn't get hurt."

"And that was wrong?"

"I know Cade meant well. And I never really hated him for it but…he didn't give me room to breathe. To make choices. Mistakes, even if I had to."

"I can understand he wanted to protect you. You were such a perky little thing. It would have been a shame if someone had hurt you, broken your heart."

Perky little thing, huh? Little Miss Sunshine. Little April. The Williams girl. She had always been treated as a vulnerable creature that needed protection. She had become so tired of it and it had been one of the reasons she'd left town. One of many reasons.

Matt glanced at her again. "How do you

think I can convince Belle I only want the best for her?"

"Oh, she knows that. That's not the problem." April began refolding the scarf. "Everyone means well, you know. But all those good intentions…"

"Hmmm." Matt nodded and focused on the road with a sad expression. "Well, I guess I don't know what to do then."

There was a deep silence. April looked out the window at the snow covered fields they were passing. It was going to be a long drive to Heartmont.

Matt released breath audibly. "I've often heard that cliché about not being able to be a father and a mother to your child. But I never felt like that. Me and Belle, we were so close. I was sure it would always be that way." He swallowed.

April bit her lip. She didn't want him to be hurting, to feel like he had failed in raising Belle. He hadn't. It was only natural that she wanted space, room to develop and find her own way in life. But to Matt it had to be like he was losing the daughter who was the center of his world after his wife had died.

"For the first time…" Matt said with difficulty, "I feel like Belle needs something I can't give her. There are things she obviously can't talk about with me. And she doesn't have a grandmother either, just a grumpy grandpa. Her words, not mine."

April said, "She does love your father very much."

"I know. And Pa loves her. You should see the two of them when they organize an Italian restaurant night. Pa bakes the pizzas and Belle does the decorations for the table." A smile relaxed his tight features for a moment. Then the tension returned and he clenched the wheel. "It's just that she doesn't have a female role model. Someone who can talk to her about things that interest her."

"Like boys," April supplied. "You wish she confided in someone who could then tell everything to you."

"No, that's not it. I'm worried she's struggling with issues and not finding a listening ear. I don't have to hear anything about it. Probably better that there are things I don't know. I mean, I can understand it's cringey to have your dad know girl's stuff. I just… I don't want her to feel…alone."

The genuine hurt in his voice touched April. She wanted to reach out and put her hand on his arm. Comfort him by letting him know she was there for him when he needed to vent.

But she shouldn't get close to Matt. That was dangerous. "I'm sure Belle isn't alone. She must have friends from school she can talk to. Girls her own age who are dealing with the same things."

"They're putting her up to no good. Not doing homework and wearing too much makeup."

Aha. April suppressed a smile. "So you're actually looking for a female role model who can act as a sort of cop, deciding what your daughter is and isn't allowed to do?"

"I'm just afraid I'm losing my little girl."

Again the honest pain in his voice grabbed April inside. She didn't want him to feel like he had failed. That he'd lose his precious daughter too. That nothing of the family he had once wanted to build would be left. The family he had sacrificed his football dreams for.

At the time when Kennedy had died in that plane crash, it had seemed so cruel, so unfair. That the woman Matt had given his all for was simply snatched away from him, leaving him heartbroken. Even thinking of it now made her throat constrict.

"Belle loves you—you know that," she said softly.

"But the peer pressure… All of those so-called friends telling her she needs to have a boyfriend too and school is boring and…" Matt glanced at April again. "I don't know what's come over her, April. She is so quiet and she looks so sad sometimes. And when I ask her about college, next year, what she'd like to study, she says she doesn't know and maybe she doesn't need a college degree and she can just stay here and work at the hotel. Now it's not like my little girl not to want to go to college. There must be something… I thought that… You helped raise her after Kennedy died. You were there for her during those first hard years. Belle clung to you. Your postcards always make her smile. She saved all of them, over the years. She loves to hear stories about life on board and… I thought that maybe you could get through to her now. Because I can't anymore." He raked his hand through his hair again.

The helpless gesture touched April's heart. She wished Ma hadn't shared her worries about who could pick up April with Matt, and he hadn't appeared at the airport. She already felt that unfortunate spark of attraction and then this emotional confession about Belle... The little girl April had cared for, almost as if...

She was her own daughter?

Yes, there had been an outing to a playground two years after Kennedy had died where Matt and Belle had been playing and April had come back from fetching something to drink and an older lady had said to her, out of the blue: "You have a lovely daughter." And looking at Matt pushing Belle on the swing, April had wished with all of her heart that Belle was her daughter and Matt was her husband and they'd be together always.

But she should have realized then she was just little April to him, that lovable tomboy from town who rode ponies and baked cookies and was just like a friend to him. A friend, not a potential love interest. That was the trouble staying in the town where you grew up: no matter how old you became, most people still saw you as a little kid, never quite as an equal. You never lost that cuteness.

Matt said, "So you think it's pretty full at the Williams ranch, huh?"

She guessed he wanted to return to an innocent topic and nodded. "Yeah. I'd really rather stay in a B&B or something but everything is fully booked."

"I have a guest room at the ranch for you."

She sat up straight as if lightning had struck her. What? Why would he offer her to stay with him?

She didn't dare look at him lest she betray her confusion and the underlying... "I thought you'd be fully booked too."

"The hotel quarters are. This would be at the house. You'd be right next to Belle's room."

April stared ahead, too flustered to respond. He'd just invited her into his home? Then another thought struck her. "Next to Belle's room?" Things clicked into place. "Wait a minute. This whole chat about you needing a female role model for her..."

"She adores you. She has kept each and every card you sent her. From all the ports your ships visited. You promised her a post-card from every destination when you left town but…" He looked at her. "I guess I thought you'd do it for a few months. Maybe a year or two? But nine years… That is being true to your word."

April flushed. How could she confess that sending those cards kept her connected to the little girl she had helped care for and the man she had been in love with? She had seen countless handsome men on the cruises. Away from work, on leave, she had sometimes dated, but no one had ever been able to match up to Matt Carpenter.

Or maybe no one had been able to match up to the romantic fantasy in her head of what Matt and she could have been if everything had been different.

She should let go of it. She had been awarded her big promotion now. She had climbed the ladder step by step, all the way from deckhand running errands to Crew Agent. When she returned to the ship, she'd get her very first uniform. With a single gold stripe on the sleeve. She'd make it two as soon as she could. The cruise world was her life. She had worked so hard for this achievement. It would mean even less time spent ashore and more responsibilities toward her team and the passengers. That was where her future lay.

Her infatuation with Matt had to end. She needed to see him for what he truly was. Just a man. Not someone special.

Certainly not the one.

So why not stay with him for a while? See him in action? Draw the conclusion that he wasn't perfect after all? That she really wasn't in love with him anymore? Because she had been away for so long, she had been able to keep her fantasy alive but it wasn't reality. And spending time with him, for real, would soon show her that. Time had gone by, people changed, Matt had to have changed as well.

In any case, April had changed. She wasn't the girl anymore who walked around all starry-eyed and in love. No, she'd face this situation with a cool head, approach the issue realistically. What were the odds of Matt ever seeing her as anything other than little April? Zero.

So how about letting the whole thing go?
Finally.

It was the last day of the year. Time to
make resolutions for the New Year that was
about to begin. What if one of her resolutions was to fall out of love with Matt Carpenter? To use her stay here to finally close
the book on that unhappy love affair that
had been more like a crush anyway, and
unrequited too?

Wasn't it sad to cling to a silly teenage
dream for so long? Wasn't it about high
time she did something about it?

Matt said, "I know you probably had a
different idea for your vacation than to stay
at my place and become friends with my
daughter but…"

"I already am friends with your daughter. And I'd love to spend time with her and
get to know her better. I want to see the
changes made to the library she wrote to
me about and play those board games she
mentioned. I want to be part of her world
for a bit. I'm sure my mother won't mind
that I come to stay at the family ranch a little later. After all, I have a six-week leave
and you know what they say about guests

outstaying their welcome… And I can still drop by to see little Barry and play with the girls."

It would be easier not to stay at the family ranch full-time at first, but she could visit, feel out the new situation with Cade's girlfriend in the mix. If she was there 24/7, she might not be able to stay rational about the past, and the last thing she wanted was to end up in a heated argument with Cade and blame him for what happened after Dad's death when she had been excluded from the decision making about the ranch's future. He'd only be hurt and probably not see what he had done wrong as he had only been protecting her and providing for the family, in his mind.

"I'd love to stay with you and connect with Belle. But I won't be your spy. And I won't tell her things you want me to convey to her. Like no makeup?"

Matt raised a hand. "No problem. I'm not even saying no makeup. I just noticed that some of her friends wear it in spades and well…"

"Matt Carpenter." April turned in her seat as far as the safety belt would let her to glare at him. "I'm willing to spend my precious vacation days at your ranch because I genuinely like your daughter and I want to find out if she's struggling with something that I can help her with. *Her*, not you. You understand?"

Matt nodded. "I understand. I won't ask you what you two discuss or… Just as long as you find out why she suddenly doesn't want to go to college anymore and you persuade her that she has to. Please?" His voice grew husky. "I gave up on my football scholarship, my chance to study and I want her to do better than me. To get somewhere in life. I want her to have all the opportunities, to become whatever she wants."

His words pierced April's heart. "I can't promise that, Matt. I want our connection to be based on mutual trust and respect. I won't invade her privacy, force her to confide in me. After all, I may have sent her postcards for nine years but that doesn't mean we know each other at all."

"She remembers that you took care of her, April. She knows you have a good heart." Matt cast her a quick smile. "You are one of the kindest, most compassionate people I know. You won't judge her. She knows that. If you just stay with us and spend time with her, she'll tell you what's bothering her."

"Maybe." April rubbed her hand over her jeans. It was suddenly a bit clammy. What was she setting herself up for? Either Belle wouldn't confide in her and then Matt's problem wouldn't be solved and the whole stay would have been pointless. Or Belle would tell her things that she couldn't tell Matt because she didn't want to break the girl's trust in her. It felt like either way she couldn't win.

And what if Belle confessed something major?

Matt said, "We can drop your luggage at my place and you can see Belle for a minute. Then you can take my car to your family to meet little Barry. If that's alright with you?"

April nodded. "Fine." She didn't want to turn up at her family's place with Matt. Ma would invite him inside for coffee and cake and his presence would be a little distracting at a moment where she wanted to focus fully on seeing her family again and meeting the newest addition. Dropping her luggage off first and then going to see her family by herself would be perfect.

Matt said, "I'm so glad you want to do this. I've been really worried about Belle lately. But having you here makes me feel better already."

"Happy to help." April forced a smile. *No pressure.*

CHAPTER TWO

WHEN THEY ARRIVED at the Carpenter hotel, the snow had formed a thin layer across the yard. To April's left were the stables where the horses waited for guests to take them on a tour, to the right stood the ranch house. Painted a deep red, it had black accents around the windows and over the door. When April had seen it for the last time, tears in her eyes had blurred the rocking chair on the porch and the table with magazines and a vase of fresh flowers. But now, in winter, those elements meant for cozy outdoor living were removed and she was glad the memories weren't so bad this way.

Or at least she could tell herself that.

Matt had rounded the car to open the door for her. He also seemed a touch nervous to have her back here. Or was it because she was going to see Belle again and he worried Belle wouldn't be as thrilled about the reunion as he wanted her to? Had he even discussed this with Belle? Or was he just bringing April here as a wonderful solution to his problem without having ascertained that his daughter actually wanted this too?

April's gut jittered with nerves as she followed Matt, who carried her suitcase up the porch steps and opened the front door. Inside a scent of burning logs from the wood in the fireplace filled the air. A couple of thirtysomethings stood at the reception desk talking to an elderly woman who was checking the screen of a whirring computer. April's gaze quickly took in the entire space from the archway that led to the kitchen, where she had often cooked meals, to the paintings of the Rockies against the back wall. A staircase with a horse's head carved at the bottom of the banister accessed the second floor, while the door to her right led to the family's private wing, where the bedrooms were. Things were comfortingly the same, although she also saw new touches in the shape of color coordinated carpets and vases. Belle's female touch?

Matt greeted the receptionist with a wave and gestured that he was going into the private wing. April followed him through the door that creaked a little. "Everything is tinder dry with the cold outside and us heating the place inside," Matt said. "I hope you don't mind the noises at night?"

"On a ship it's never quiet. I sleep through it all." April looked ahead to the door that had led to Belle's bedroom. Last time she was here it had been a typical girl's room with a pink table and chairs, a princess corner and a bed full of stuffed animals. Now it had to be completely different. A young lady's domain where maybe no one else was welcome?

How could Matt simply assume Belle would open up to her? She had been away for so long…

Matt opened the door into the bedroom beside Belle's and gestured. "Here we are. I hope it meets with your approval."

She passed him to move inside, her arm brushing his. She tried to ignore the trickle of excitement in her chest. Spending time with him here would soon feel normal and she could finally see him as just some guy she used to know.

The room's walls were painted butter yellow and the bed was decked out in a bright blue duvet and pillows. On top of one pillow was a purple plastic bag of...

April walked over and picked it up. Weighing it on her palm, she turned to Matt. "Chocolate coated raisins? You remembered?" As she said it, she realized that he couldn't have put these here before he had left. He had told her that he had gone to her family's ranch and then learned she was coming home today... So how had these ended up in her room?

"I did," a voice said.

April looked at the girl in the doorway. Over the years she had seen the occasional photo of Belle, and in the last few months they had even videocalled a few times. But seeing someone in person was very different. It felt like a momentous occasion, and April realized she longed to reconnect with the past she had left behind.

Belle's dark hair, exactly the same color as Matt's, was brushed back and held in place with a velvet headband. She wore jeans and a dark blue cardigan over a white blouse. She had grown taller and seemed more self-assured, but April could still recognize so much of the little girl she had loved. She smiled widely. "Belle! So good to see you. How have you been?"

"Okay." Belle nodded and shuffled her feet. "I hope you still like those?" She nodded at the bag in April's hands. "Dad texted Grandpa he wasn't coming home for hours because he was picking someone up at the airport and to get the guest room ready… I knew he had gone to the Williams ranch for supplies so I put two and two together. I really hoped it was you. I bought those especially at the mercantile."

Matt rolled his eyes at his daughter. "Did you read Grandpa's texts?"

"He told me what it said. Do you really think he made this bed? I did." Belle put her hands on her hips. "Grandpa couldn't get a duvet on straight if his life depended on it."

Matt shook his head but his eyes betrayed he was laughing inside.

"Thanks," April said, holding up the chocolate coated raisins. "I do still love them and I appreciate you went out especially to get them for me."

Belle nodded seriously. "It must be weird to be back. You haven't been here for so long."

April wasn't sure what Belle was feeling now. Regret that she hadn't come before? Or curiosity that she was suddenly willing to come? Perhaps even a bit of…suspicion? Was she onto her father's plan?

April said hurriedly, "You know, on the Williams ranch there is so much bustle. Gina with her kids, Cade's girlfriend. I'd rather have some peace and quiet to, uh, unwind after a busy season. Besides, I really wanted to catch up with you. I have some fab news to tell you."

"Oh really?" Belle seemed interested now. "But don't you have to see your family first? I guess they will be waiting for you."

"We decided it would be handy to drop the luggage here first." Matt explained to Belle and held out the SUV's key to April. "Take my car and go see them."

"But you have to be back in time to change for the party." Belle took two steps toward April and eyed her earnestly. "You will come to the party, won't you?"

"Of course."

From deeper inside the house someone hollered Matt's name.

"That's Grandpa." Belle sighed. "He's having trouble changing a light bulb."

"I told him not to clamber onto ladders when I'm out." Matt hurried away.

Belle smiled at April. "Thanks for your last two postcards. I've never seen one of an antique cannery before."

"Well, I try to pick postcards that don't look too similar to ones I already sent. I accompanied an elderly lady who felt a little uncertain on the tour to the cannery and then discovered they sold the cards in a small shop. It was very authentic. I also took photos I can show you later."

"Do you remember every card you sent me?" It seemed to be a genuine question, not a tease.

April tilted her head. "Well, I can't claim to have a perfect memory, but I do have to pay attention to a lot of details in my work, remember a lot of names and timetables, so I guess my ability to recall information is better than most people's." She shrugged. "Maybe you think postcards are old-fashioned and I could simply text you a photo?"

"Uh-uh. Come and look." Belle made an inviting gesture for her to come along into the corridor. She opened the door into her own room and waved April in.

Once through the doorway April stopped and stared. On all walls of the room were postcards. Pinned to corkboards, or framed, turned into collages. Images from all the destinations she had been to: tropical harbors and icy panoramas, botanical gardens and temple ruins. They formed a colorful window onto the world.

A bookcase covered the far wall and a desk held more books and papers. Also a framed photograph of Matt, Kennedy and little Belle, taken on her fourth birthday, a few weeks before the plane crash that had ripped Kennedy away from them.

April's gaze lingered on their faces, their happiness captured in these carefree moments as a family. It was an old photo, part of a past long gone, but to Belle it had to have a very special meaning. It was her family, a memory of the mother she had lost too soon.

Belle said, "I kept all your postcards. I often look at them and wish I could see those places for myself."

"Maybe you can sometime. Start closer to home and then work your way around the world." As she said it, April realized Matt would probably not welcome her encouraging his daughter to travel the world.

Belle's eyes turned down. "It's just a bit of fantasizing in bed at night. Not something I'd really do. I like it here in Heartmont. They need me at the library. They're short on volunteers because most people think it's boring, but I really like it. I love books."

"Me too." April's phone pinged and she checked the screen. "My mother. She wants to know if I've landed safely. I should probably have let her know sooner."

"Go surprise her in person." Belle came over and pulled the bag of raisins from April. "I'll put this back in your room. You go."

April nodded and left the house.

WHEN SHE DROVE Matt's SUV into the yard of her childhood home, the first thing she saw were Gina's five-year-old twins frolicking in the snow. Ann, the more quiet of the two, was carefully forming snow into a ball to become the head of a snowman whose body was already in place in front of the porch. Stacey, the wild one, collected hands full of snow to throw at someone who just emerged from the barn.

Cade.

April felt the tension roll through her body, grabbing her muscles and freezing the smile on her face. She found it hard to see her brother ever since he'd chosen not to ask her opinion about the ranch's future after Dad's sudden death. Apparently it had been self-evident to Cade that he would take over, so he hadn't bothered to ask her whether she'd like to join in.

It still hurt no matter how successful she'd been in her own work. She had considered this place her home but he hadn't asked her to be a part of the decisions about the future of it.

Cade ignored Stacey's attacks and came over to the vehicle. A frown hovered over his eyes as he pulled the door open. "April… Why are you driving Carpenter's car?"

Carpenter he called him. Not Matt. Cade

had never liked Matt for some reason April couldn't quite fathom. Unless it was because Cade hadn't wanted her to befriend a widower with a young daughter? Had he thought that it might lead to complications down the road?

Annoyance raced through her veins. Cade always thought he could decide for her.

"Matt was kind enough to pick me up from the airport. Ma asked him to. He took me to the ranch hotel to drop my things and then offered the use of the SUV to me to get here. And you might have said, 'Hello, April, nice to see you.'"

Her last words seemed lost on Cade who kept staring at her with that worried frown. "You dropped your things at his place? You're going to stay there? Why? We have plenty of room here."

"I know that, but after a long stretch on board I really need a bit of time and space to myself. Besides, I have a six week leave so there's plenty of time for me to come and stay with you later." She forced a smile and put her hand on his arm. "Try to understand."

His expression told her he didn't, or didn't

want to, but further conversation about this painful topic was prevented when a sporty-looking blonde woman walked over to them waving an arm. Her brown eyes shone with a warm glow as she came to stand beside Cade. "Hello. You must be April. You look a lot like Gina. I'm Lily."

"Pleased to meet you," April mumbled.

She registered the disappointment in Cade's features at her lukewarm response to his girlfriend. The one who had changed everything for everyone, remember?

April gave herself a virtual kick and hugged Lily. She forced enthusiasm into her voice when she said, "I've heard so much about you. I can't tell you how happy I am that my big brother finally met his match. He needs someone to, uh…steer him the other way once in a while."

"What's that supposed to mean?" Cade inquired.

Lily slapped at him. "You stay out of it. I know exactly what April is driving at and I agree." She gave April a megawatt smile. "I'm so glad to meet you too. It's nice to be together on the last day of the year. Are you coming to the party tonight? We've done quite a bit of organizing for it. It's going to be amazing."

"You shouldn't say that about your own party," Cade warned her. "Besides, April had a long flight out here from Miami and might not feel like company all evening."

She was surprised he was taking that into account. Maybe he was more considerate than she gave him credit for. Or was he merely preparing Lily for the disappointment when April would decline her invitation to come?

"Auntie Lily," Stacey cried, "come and look at our snowman." She had helped Ann to put the head on the body.

The girls hadn't shown any interest in April. That hurt but she told herself that they hadn't seen much of her over the years and perhaps didn't even recognize her all wrapped up against the cold. Besides, they were working so hard on their snowman that they were probably oblivious to everything else.

"Auntie Lily!" Stacey insisted.

"Coming," Lily called back. She gave Cade a quick squeeze on the arm.

It was weird to see someone who was a

perfect stranger to April be so close with her brother. And to see Cade smile so tenderly while he watched his girlfriend walk away with his nieces. The spark between him and Lily was obvious.

For a moment April wondered why falling in love seemed to be easy for everyone but her. Even for her taciturn, workaholic brother who never dated and to her knowledge avoided conversation about anything personal whenever he could. How had these two ever found common ground?

Then she dismissed the thought and smiled at Cade. "She looks like a really nice person."

"You could have come to meet her before. Or to see the baby right after he was born."

"You know that I can't just leave my ship at will. I have limited time off." *And that is about to become even less with my promotion.* She didn't want to mention that now. Cade wouldn't be happy. He had never liked her working far away from home. He thought that…

This was the place where she belonged?

Then why hadn't he involved her more so she had felt like he wanted her to stay?

She shook her head in an attempt to break the spiral of thoughts. "I'm glad to be here now, Cade. To meet Lily and see Gina's little boy."

Cade's eyes got a besotted look. "He's the most perfect little thing you've ever seen."

"Little? I thought he was three months old already."

"Yes, he is growing up fast." Cade nodded, still grinning. "You'll find him inside with his mom and his grandmother fussing over him." He gestured at the house. "Go in and surprise them."

As she was about to walk away, he added, almost as an afterthought, "It's good to have you back."

April nodded and hurried to the house. The cold wind breathed down her neck and she pulled up her shoulders. A snowflake got into her eye, or something like that to explain the burn she felt there. She pushed the door open and stood in the hallway breathing deep. She was home again. It hurt and at the same time she was glad she had come. She couldn't avoid it forever. She needed to work through complicated feelings and get her life on track. Now more than ever.

She walked softly through the corridor toward the kitchen area. Rosie the Border collie came up to her, her head poised to break into excited barking. April raised her hand to her mouth fast to tell the dog to stay quiet. As a working dog, Rosie was trained to recognize hand signals and follow leads even if these went against her instinct. She pushed her snout against April's other hand to express her happiness at seeing her, but didn't make a sound. April petted the dog's head and then moved farther toward the kitchen on tiptoe.

Gina sat in the leather club chair by the fireplace, gazing down at the baby. He lay in the crook of her arm, all bundled up against the chill of December. Ma stood beside Gina, head bowed to look at her grandson, an exalted expression on her face.

April stopped. The stab inside her was sharp and painful. They were family; they had family, and she was all alone. At least that was how it felt right now, standing outside the circle of warmth from the fire, looking in on their happiness. Perhaps that was why she had taken Matt's offer to stay with him. To avoid living here for weeks on end and seeing how close everyone was, while she no longer was a part of that. She had made other choices; she lived a vastly different life, away from the community at the ranch and in town.

She knew her family loved her despite her departure and that she was most welcome here, and still…she felt locked out. Excluded. Perhaps it only took a cheerful hello to break the painful tension and be invited into their midst. Still, she'd struggle with the feelings inside. Because she had once wanted to sit like Gina sat there, with her baby in her arms, her mother fussing over the infant and then…her husband coming through the door and locking them in his arms. Now she was a single career woman and…she could never quite figure out if she was totally happy with that or still regretted it a little. And if it was the latter, if she should act on that feeling.

A board creaked and Ma looked up. Her eyes rested on April for a few moments as if not quite sure what she saw. Or if she was seeing it right. Then a wide smile spread across her features and she came for April, arms wide open. April disappeared into her mother's hug. She closed her eyes and relished the warmth and security of that moment. There was nothing quite like being held by your mother. Even if you were all grown up now.

Ma grabbed her by the shoulders and said, "You're here. At last. Let me look at you. You look well. I'm glad… I worried you were working too hard. And not even home for Christmas." She shook her head. "I know you love your work, April, but you have so little time off. Always working on holidays."

Another one who wouldn't be happy with her promotion, April thought with a sad sigh inside.

Ma said, "But anyway, you're here now. I'm so glad you could make it right before the party tonight. You have to come."

"I already agreed to that." April kissed her mother on the cheek. "Now let me have a look at my nephew." She smiled at Gina, who had risen from the chair, carefully holding the sleeping baby against her. April closed the distance and smiled down on the little face. She reached out and touched one of his cheeks with her pinkie. "He's so tiny."

"He was much tinier," Gina assured her. "Do you want to hold him?"

"Yes, sit down here," Ma said, pointing at the other chair, "and I will make you some hot chocolate with banana bread."

April sank into the chair and Gina lowered the baby into her arms. April was worried he'd notice he wasn't with his mother anymore and would wake up and start crying, but he slept through it all, one small hand pushed against his face.

"Little Barry," Gina whispered. Her expression was joyful and sad at the same time. She had to be thinking of her husband the baby was named after. He had never held his son in his arms. He had died before Barry was born, in a tragic skiing accident. "The twins are so happy with their baby brother."

"Although Stacey feels…" Ma said from the counter where she was heating the milk for the chocolate, "…that he cries a lot."

All three of them laughed softly. April inhaled the scent of baby powder, logs in the fireplace, kitchen spices and baked sweetness. She was home. It might not always be easy to come here, but still it was right that she had decided to make the trip now. She had a place here, among the people she loved and who loved her back, despite the disagreements between them. It need not be perfect as long as it was real.

"Did you come in Matt's SUV?" Ma asked, nodding out the window.

April shrugged. "That seemed easiest. I don't have a car here. I don't have a car, period." She laughed softly. "I tend to forget about it as I simply don't need it most of the time." She waited a moment. Better bite the bullet straight away. "I'll be staying with Matt. He offered and…well, it seemed convenient. You have a lot going on here as it is and I need a bit of quiet and space to unwind after the busy season on the ship."

Gina hitched a brow. "Stay with Matt? Not here? Why?" She looked at Ma as if wanting support in objecting to this decision.

But Ma said, "If you think it's better,

April, it's fine with me." She carried the hot chocolate over to her and put a plate with a slice of banana bread beside it. "There you go. Enjoy."

"Let me have Barry again," Gina said and took the baby out of April's arms.

It felt empty a moment. April quickly picked up the hot chocolate and blew to cool the surface. "I saw Lily briefly. She seems nice."

"She's amazing," Gina gushed. "I'm so glad she got together with Cade. It couldn't be better."

Once Lily married Cade and this became her house, there would be even less room for April. For her ideas about the ranch. None of the family asked her what she thought, how she felt. Maybe it was just assumed she didn't mind what happened to the ranch because she was always away?

Gina said, "Lily organized most of the New Year's Eve party too. It's at the mayor's place. There are heated party tents behind his house and there will be music, dancing…"

Could she get a dance with Matt?

For a moment she imagined what it would

be like to be in his arms, soaking up those precious minutes and keeping them in her heart always.

But that might not be too smart. After all, she was trying to fall out of love with him, not into it. Her stay at the ranch hotel had to prove to her that Matt Carpenter was just a normal man, who might be handsome but also had very irritating habits, and that he was certainly not the dream partner she had made him out to be.

"Great food, and fireworks." Gina was still extolling the virtues of Lily's party. "I don't think we've ever had such a wonderful party here before. Oh, he's starting to fuss a bit. Maybe I'd better put him in his crib so he can sleep in peace. Yeah, little man… Come on." She carried the baby out of the kitchen.

Rosie came to lie beside April's chair looking up at her with attentive amber eyes. It was as if the dog was asking, "How are you?"

Ma said, "You mustn't blame Gina for thinking the world of Lily. Lily helped out at the pizzeria when the twins were born."

The pizzeria had initially belonged to

Barry's parents and Barry had taken over when he married Gina so the income from the restaurant could support their family.

Ma continued, "She was also a great support to her after Barry had his skiing accident and died. When all the debts came to light and Gina was forced to sell everything she owned, Lily helped her with debt counseling and all. Those two are close like sisters."

Exactly, April thought, *Gina and I are sisters but she's not that close with me.*

Maybe that's my own fault? I was away too often. Even after Barry died. I should have been there for Gina, instead of Lily picking up the pieces. But I just didn't know what to say, how to comfort her, or face her crying girls. I hid behind work and...

In her job she was always the problem solver. In the past, with Matt's grief over Kennedy, she had known how to face it, head-on, and help him. But when it came to her own family, she was often at a loss what to do. How to reach them. It was too personal and then she clammed up. Biting her lip, she said nothing, just nursed her hot chocolate.

Ma continued, "Gina needs all the help she can get now. With three children and no husband. Trying to get her life back on track again after all the financial trouble. She's looking for a job in town but it isn't easy in winter. People who normally work the land take whatever is available at restaurants and in shops."

"I know, Ma." *I grew up here.* "I know how hard the winter season is on everyone. But I'm sure Gina will find something suitable in due time. And I'm glad for her that Lily helps her. And I'm glad for Cade he found someone to be with. He worked too hard."

"So you're glad and glad and…" Ma came to stand at her chair, giving her a probing look. "But you're not coming to stay here."

"Matt offered to have me at the hotel and well, I had a feeling he had an ulterior motive." She wasn't about to tell Ma what Matt had said. That would be insensitive toward him and Belle. "Maybe he wants me to give him some feedback about the hotel? You know, a few pointers? I do work in customer service, so to speak."

"Aha." Ma nodded with a half smile. "So it is a business arrangement."

"Definitely." April took a large sip of hot chocolate and burned her tongue. But she had to distract her mother. "I have some wonderful news to share with you." She clenched the mug as she said, "I got promoted. I'm a one-stripe officer now. I'll get my very own uniform."

Ma looked down at her and April caught the momentary flash of disappointment. As if Ma had expected other news. *I'm leaving the cruise business? I'm going back to shore?*

Or: I found someone? I'm dating? It's serious?

Ma leaned down and hugged her, mug and all. "Congratulations. You worked so hard for that. Got passed over several times."

"Don't remind me." April grimaced. "I just want to embrace the feeling I finally made it."

"Made what?" Cade asked. He came in, rubbing his hands. There was a light powdering of snow in his hair. Lily followed, her arms wrapped around the twins who were chattering about their snowman. As soon as they spied April, Stacey clapped her hands together. "You came. I asked Gran last week if you'd come. She said she didn't know."

"It was a surprise," April said.

Stacey beamed. "Last time you brought us presents. Do you have presents now?"

Ann poked her with an elbow. "It's not polite to ask about presents."

Ma suppressed laughter. Stacey said indignantly, "You want presents too. Don't say you don't." She pulled the snowy woolen hat off her sister's head. Ann reached out to tug at Stacey's scarf.

"Girls, girls, that's enough," Ma said. "Take off your snowy clothes in the hallway and then come back to give April a good hug."

Still tugging at each other, the twins ran off. Gina, who just came back from putting Barry to bed, followed to help them wriggle out of their wet coats.

Cade kept looking at April with a slight frown. "Why did you say you made it?"

"I got promoted," April said. "To Crew Agent. It's a job in uniform, one gold stripe.

And with good prospects of becoming Crew Manager later."

"Well done," Lily enthused, "congratulations." She came over and hugged April. Over Lily's shoulder she looked at Cade. She saw the same mixed reaction as her mother's. They had to swallow down some sort of disappointment before they could be happy for her. But why? What else did they think she could do? Sit here as the fifth wheel on the wagon? She needed her own life. Her own ambitions and career.

"Well done, sis." Cade hugged her. For a moment she savored the warmth of his embrace. As he wasn't big on compliments, it meant all the more to her.

"Do you also want hot chocolate?" Ma asked. Cade nodded and she turned to the sink.

The twins ran back in and came over to April who sank to her knees to hug and kiss them. Their cheeks were cold from playing outside. She ached for those carefree childhood moments when life was so perfect, with a freshly made snowman outside and hot chocolate being prepared inside. Invited by Ma, the twins clambered on stools to help make it. Lily gently supervised them to ensure the cacao powder ended up in the milk instead of on the sink. She was at home here, April thought.

Cade looked her in the eye. He asked in a low voice, "Are you sure this is what you want?"

"What?"

"Getting a uniform and all. I…guess I have to adjust to the idea that you think one gold stripe on your sleeve is important."

A need to defend herself made her say, sharper than intended, "I worked very hard for this promotion. Got passed over several times. I deserve this."

"Of course. I'm not saying you don't…"

"Never mind, Cade." April stepped back, forcing herself to keep smiling. "As long as I know what I'm doing with my life…"

"I don't mean to say it's wrong. Just… you used to love animals and wanted to live in a small community forever. The cruise ship business is a world away from that."

"When you grow up, dreams change." April shrugged. "I'm happy now." She knew deep inside that she wasn't being perfectly honest with him. She was happy with her work, yes, and the promotion was the proudest moment of her life. But she wasn't fully truly happy. The moments holding little Barry in her arms had made that crystal clear. She ached for something she had never had, something just out of reach. She wasn't fully happy because of Matt, of what she believed could have been but hadn't materialized.

She had to get rid of that last bit of attachment to the old dream.

CHAPTER THREE

APRIL HAD MORE hot chocolate and banana bread with the family but said she wouldn't have dinner with them as she wanted to have a bit of time to herself before the New Year's Eve party started. Ma seemed pleased she would attend, and Lily said she was looking forward to chatting more then and getting to know her better. April made herself a silent promise to also talk with Cade at the party. The light mood might help them to have a conversation without misunderstanding each other and building tension instead of alleviating it.

Trying to keep everyone's interests in mind was a balancing act and she was half relieved to be able to dive into the SUV and drive back to the hotel. As soon as she entered the hallway, Belle came to her with a hesitant smile. "I thought you had forgotten all about me. You must have been happy to see your family again. The party starts at eight thirty. Still time to eat something. I can make pizza." She gave April a hopeful look. "You used to cook for me—now let me do that for you."

"Sure, fine with me," April added as she followed the girl through the door into the kitchen. Her plan to lie down for a bit went out the window, but she was used to being available whenever people needed her and to long hours on her feet. She could do this.

She wanted to do this, because she cared for Belle. "Where is your father?"

"To his annoyance he couldn't get the bulb fixed either. He went out to get some little tool he needs." Belle shrugged. "If he's done, he'll come looking for food."

"Don't you eat together?" April asked. "I mean, I thought the benefit of living under a single roof with three generations was that you always have company."

"Too much company at times," Belle said, rolling her eyes. She opened a huge freezer and asked, "What do you like? Salami, Hawaiian, chicken, four cheeses…"

"You sound like a pizzeria."

"We all love pizza so we have plenty in stock."

"Hawaiian for me. I'm firmly in camp Pineapple On Pizza Is The Best." April took a seat on a stool at the high wooden bar. "Does your father ever cook? I mean, I seem to remember he was learning how to."

"Oh, he can cook pretty decently." Belle smiled at her. "And I cook a lot too. I love trying new things. But sometimes we're just tired and we take the easy way, you know."

April nodded. She stopped herself from scanning the entire area for little changes since she had last been here. She had to stop thinking about the past. It was over and done with.

"So what are you wearing to the party?" Belle asked after she had put the pizza in the oven.

April frowned. "What's the dress code? I mean, are we supposed to dress up or keep it casual? After all, it's just a town get-together."

"It's New Year's Eve! We do need something festive. You sound just like Dad. He thought he could get away with a clean shirt and jeans. I told him he does need to look smart."

Matt in a suit and tie? Dangerous. "I guess he figures the party's informal and he doesn't want to stand out."

"It's not informal. At least, I'm dressing up. Can you help me with my makeup? Just a few pointers." Belle came over and studied April's face. "You're lucky that you look good without much makeup. I have a very ordinary and boring face."

"I wouldn't say that."

"I think so." Belle ambled past the sink, tapping a finger on the counter every other step. "I never get asked out for a date. That must mean something." She looked up at April. "Do you get asked for dates a lot on the cruise ship?"

"I work there. I'm not allowed to date passengers."

"Oh. But what if you met someone and you fell head over heels in love?"

"I don't look at passengers that way." April leaned her chin in her hand. "It's all a matter of reminding yourself that you have to be professional about that. Besides, I don't think I believe in love at first sight either. I think you sort of…fall for some-one by getting to know them. Being around them and starting to see all the good things about them."

"Hmmm." Belle nodded pensively. "Still, will you help me with my makeup? If you say it's okay, Dad won't mind so much. He hates me looking at tutorials online. He thinks I'm too young for it. I'm sixteen! I bet you could have makeup when you were sixteen."

"Well, as a matter of fact I didn't care much for makeup when I was sixteen. I was always in the stables, looking after the animals at the ranch and horse riding. I was what you call a tomboy. Sometimes I think I still am." April grinned at Belle. "You know, on the cruise ship I play the glammed up attendant—I have to look im-peccable for the guests but… I'm still a country girl at heart." As she said it she knew it was true. She needn't lie for Belle's sake. She really didn't care all that much for her looks.

"Do you miss it here when you're away?" Belle asked. She leaned back against the counter now, a serious look on her face. It was so strange to see this young woman and remember the little girl April had sheltered in her arms.

"I don't have much time to miss it. I'm on my feet eleven hours a day."

"That much? Is that even allowed?"

"It's a given in the industry. You have to work hard and always smile and be friendly. And you can never ever feel sorry for yourself." April gestured with her free hand. "It worked brilliantly for me when I was first on a trip. I didn't have time to think of home and…feel lonely. I was just very tired at night and fell asleep right away. I was a deckhand then—that means you have to make sure chairs on the sun decks are in place and clean, that there are towels at the pool or that people can find locations. You have to do a lot of menial work and you can never say no when you get an assignment. It's about showing you know how to work and deal with difficult passengers and… People often have an ideal image of working on a cruise ship. Like you work a few hours and then you get off and you watch the sunset or you go see a movie. But you're not allowed to lounge in the areas for the guests. We do have a recreational area of our own, for the staff, but we can't enjoy all the luxuries the passengers have. It's like a hotel, really. If you work there as a waiter, you can't dine yourself."

Belle nodded. "That makes sense. But don't you ever feel excluded?"

"No, I got used to it quickly. I guess it helped that I never had much luxury at home. I never felt like I deserved it. It's more of a glittery foreign world I look in on but am not really a part of."

A delicious smell was spreading from the oven and Belle started to get plates and napkins for them. "Maybe we can email and text more once you're on the ship again? I like it when you let me know where you are and what the highlights of the area are."

"That's good to hear. You have been a bit quiet lately. I thought maybe…well, you were busy with other things now. School and then the library…"

"I sat down to write a few times but I couldn't find the right words." Belle bit her lip as she fetched glasses. "Do you want water or juice?"

"Water. I guess we'll be offered drinks later tonight so water is best for now."

"Right." Belle filled both glasses at the tap.

"So why couldn't you find the right words?" April asked as Belle put the glass in front of her.

"I don't know. I thought maybe life here was boring to you." It sounded much like an excuse. Was Matt right? Was Belle worried about something she couldn't share with anyone?

"I always love hearing from you. And I wouldn't call life here boring. You can always safely contact me."

"What's that delicious smell?" Matt came in. His hair looked wet from the snow. He shrugged out of a damp fleece jacket and hung it over a chair to dry. She remembered he had always left loads of stuff in his wake. Not expecting anyone to clean up after him, because he simply didn't see that there was anything there to clean up. She suppressed a smile.

"Pizza for April and me," Belle explained.

"Can I have some? Just one slice? I've been running around all afternoon." Matt squeezed his daughter's shoulder in passing. He smiled at April. "Hi there. How were things on the Williams ranch?"

"I saw my little nephew for the first time. I had seen photos of course but…"

"…that's not the same thing." Matt completed the sentence for her. He sat down and his aftershave wafted her way. She wished she had avoided this cozy little scene.

"I'm glad Gina is doing better." She kept talking to stop the memories from crowding her. "And the girls looked so happy. They love Lily."

"Sorry you accepted my invitation to stay here?" Matt's brown eyes probed hers.

April felt a treacherous blush creep up her cheeks. "Not at all. It's quieter here and I need that to unwind." She kept repeating that weak excuse.

Belle said, "Dad, don't make her feel like she should have stayed with her family." She put a plate with a slice of pizza in front of him with an indignant thud. "Here is much better. Babies cry all the time. Especially at night."

"Oh, I forgot all about that," Matt said with a grin. He lifted the pizza slice and took a bite.

Belle distributed slices to April and herself and they ate. There was a peaceful quiet in the kitchen. A sort of harmonious atmosphere of…belonging?

April chewed hard on her pizza. She so didn't want this kind of intimacy to happen. The growing feeling she had a deeper connection with these two. With Belle but also with her handsome father. She needed to find something about Matt that she didn't like. To realize he was the hero from a teenage fantasy, not a man she could truly love.

But as she studied him while he tucked into the pizza with relish, she realized he was still as good-looking and charming as ever. As down to earth and dependable. He had picked her up and driven her here safely and arranged for her to stay in the guest room and…

There was nothing she didn't like about this homecoming.

Except for the fact that it interfered with all her carefully laid plans.

MATT LOOKED UP and found April studying him with an intensity that punched his gut. She'd always had a way of probing him, searching below the surface. He recalled how she had been one of very few people who had honestly addressed his grief with him. Who had talked to him about the loss of Kennedy. Other people had carefully avoided the topic, afraid of his response. But not little April.

She had been an extraordinary girl.

Belle's phone pinged and she looked at the screen. "It's Madelyn calling. I have to take this." She hurried from the kitchen.

"Why can't she take it with us present?" Matt asked April. "I always have a feeling these calls are super secret."

"A little privacy never goes amiss." April rubbed her fingers on her napkin. "You should give her some space to breathe, Matt. Otherwise you'll only alienate her."

He nodded. He wanted to ask her if she had already been able to ask some questions, find out something significant, but it was too soon. He had to be more patient. But there was this jittery restless feeling inside him that he couldn't quite explain. As if he had to be on guard. As if there was… risk here.

"What did your mother say when you walked in?" he queried for distraction.

"She was happy to see me of course. Everyone was." April sounded a little lost, moving the last bite of pizza around on her plate. He had asked her in the car if she didn't like to come home. He sensed a reluctance there and he wondered what it was. If it had anything to do with him. He knew he had treated her unfairly by sending her away. But it had been so complicated. If he had explained it to her, he might have easily been misunderstood. Her brother had already thought the worst of him. Had pressured him to let his little sister go. Because he was taking up too much of her time and...

Matt frowned a moment. He didn't want to go there. He had let April leave and apparently it had been the right decision because she had started working on a cruise ship shortly after and had been doing so ever since. She loved traveling, was cut out for customer service...

It had all turned out well. For everyone.

Belle came back in. "Madelyn is coming to the party in a dress with sequins. A real fancy thing. I told you I needed something more than a white blouse and skirt."

"You're sixteen. Nobody expects you to come all dressed up to a town party," Matt replied automatically.

"Madelyn expects me to. She's the leader of the pack in school. She'll have all her friends with her, and they'll make fun of me." Belle looked about ready to burst into tears. "I don't want to go."

"Of course you're going," he said, half rising from his bar stool. "You don't have to listen to those girls. They aren't your friends anyway."

"You don't understand." Belle ran from the kitchen, clutching her phone.

Matt looked at April. She pursed her lips.

He lowered his tense shoulders and sighed. "Say it. Tell me what grade I'm getting for my parenting skills in this situation. Judging by your expression, it won't be pretty."

April smiled now. "Look, Matt, you could at least consider her dilemma. Maybe these girls aren't her friends, but obviously they are an important factor in her school life. I remember those types. The popular girls who always have the newest back-pack or the best clothes and they make fun of people who don't. Belle might not even want to be in their circle, but she also doesn't want them to make her the center of attention because she doesn't fit in."

Matt tried to relax the kinks in his neck. "And what do I do then?"

"Ask her what she wants to wear."

"Then I'll end up with a daughter in a super tight glittery dress with a ton of makeup on her face."

"Look…" April slipped off her stool. "Let me talk to her. I can help her dress up in a way so that she feels good about herself and doesn't have to worry about these girls."

"Uh…" Matt was suddenly not certain if this was a good idea or not. He didn't know what April had in mind and… Should he simply trust her judgment?

"I'm on it." April walked away. Matt stared at the plate where the last bite of her pizza still lay. She was selflessly throwing herself into his parental troubles. She had to have come here hoping for quiet and a time to relax. Now, instead of her being able to rest up before leaving for the party, she had to discuss a complicated subject with his daughter. He felt guilty for landing April with a job during her vacation. Still she had responded well to his request and…

He rubbed his forehead and got himself a glass of water. He just hoped April could find the antidote to Belle's blues.

APRIL KNOCKED ON the bedroom door. "Belle? It's me. Can I come in?"

Belle's voice came after a short silence. "Yeah."

April opened the door and stepped across the threshold. Belle lay on her bed, on her back, staring up at the ceiling. Her eyes were dry. She hadn't been crying or anything. April was relieved to see it. It would have been difficult to handle tears so soon after her arrival, while they still had to build their bond. But if Belle was open to a talk about the dilemma, April might be able to help.

She closed the door and walked over. "Are you okay?"

"Yeah. Fine. Those girls are really not

that interesting. It's just that… Madelyn always has the best clothes and the newest phone and she thinks she's so special." Belle rolled her eyes. "It's really pathetic, you know."

"I guess all girls your age are insecure." April sat on the edge of the bed. "They just want to be accepted. And if you have nice stuff, it helps to impress friends. But I bet we can find something that'll work in your wardrobe."

"I wish I had a mother." Belle stared at the ceiling. "Then I could go shopping with her and she'd tell me what looked good on me. Dad always thinks it's not okay unless it's baggy jeans and some sweater I drown in."

"What do you want to wear?" April asked. "I mean, not because of Madelyn and her gang. But what you, yourself, really want."

Belle took a deep breath. "I wish I knew what I have to wear to make Bobby see me."

"Bobby?"

Belle shot upright and beamed at April. "He's the cutest boy in school. He's not too handsome you know, not slick or anything.

Just good-looking and kind of shy. He likes books like me. He's often at the library. I want to say hi and ask if I can recommend a book but it would come out wrong."

"How wrong?"

"Well, all squeaky. I want to talk to him in a natural way, not sound like my foot got caught under the door."

April had to smile. "I'm sure it won't be that bad."

"Won't it? What did you say to the guy you had a crush on? You must have had a crush on someone when you were my age. What did you say?"

April laughed softly. "I never said anything. I was too scared."

"See. That's what I mean. Now how will I ever get him to notice me before someone else snatches him? I guess all the other girls can see how great he is too." She took a deep breath. "I mean, it's true that Madelyn and her gang are after other boys, like Dean and Paul, because they play football and all, and Bobby doesn't…but…they can't fail to see he's the cutest, right?"

"Maybe he's not on their radar?"

"Yet." Belle stared at April with a desperate look. "I have to do something. Get him to notice me."

"I guess what you really need is to talk with him. Will he be at the party tonight?"

"Sure. But I'm not going to talk to him. No way."

Belle crawled backward on the bed as if avoiding a snarling tiger. She leaned against the headboard, clenching her hands together.

"Oh yes you are. Because we are going to rehearse a nice conversation." April got up from the bed and pointed at the closet doors. "Can we have a look at your clothes to see what might work tonight? It doesn't need to be super fancy—that is fake. You are you, remember? But we can glam it up. Trust me."

Belle gave her a doubtful look. "Can we?"

"Show me what you had decided on. You said something about a white blouse with a skirt?"

"I don't even like skirts. I'd rather just wear jeans. But it's a party."

"Don't you have black pants made of something like velvet… A bit festive?"

They went through Belle's wardrobe

together and found a pair of black pants that Belle had bought but never worn before. They put a white blouse on top and a sleeveless jacket with embroidery. Then April ran to her room to get something and offered it to Belle with a grin. "Here is a pair of very special earrings."

Belle looked at the palm of her hand where two earrings lay. Formed like flowers, they were filled with small rhinestones that sparkled in the light. "They are gorgeous," she breathed.

"We're going to put your hair up and then the earrings will get even more attention. Let me give it a go." April directed Belle to her dressing table and sat her down. She picked up a brush and brushed Belle's long hair. It was so soft under her touch. Her throat constricted thinking of the many times she had done Belle's hair when she had been a little girl. She had felt so connected to her, so protective of her. And Belle had loved her in return. Now looking at the serious face of the young woman in the mirror, April wished she really knew her, knew what she dreamt of or what she was worried about. That they could be friends and...

She swallowed hard and put the brush down, gathered up Belle's hair and twisted it. She draped the bundle against Belle's head. "I want to pin it here and here. How do you like it?"

"It's very different. Mature." Belle grinned at her in the reflection. "I love it."

April nodded. "I need a few clips or things to secure it with."

"In that little box." Belle looked at the earrings that rested on the dressing table. "Are you sure I can wear those? Don't you want to wear them yourself?"

"I've got lots of earrings. You can use them for tonight."

"Thanks, you're the best."

April carefully pinned the hair in place and then said, "Now about makeup... I think the earrings should get full attention, don't you? So we can better keep your makeup low key and natural. A bit of mascara and a little shine on your lips."

Belle readily agreed and looked for the mascara in her makeup purse. "I can't believe it's me," she gushed turning her head to look at herself from all angles. "The girls will be so surprised."

"I thought it was about Bobby," April observed quietly.

"Yes, of course." Now Belle flushed. "I guess I…I want him to notice me, but what if he does and comes over and I have to talk to him? I'm sure I can't. I will clam up and he'll think I don't even like him."

"It'll be alright." April squeezed her shoulder. "Trust me. Now hold still as I do your mascara."

MATT HAD CHANGED into a clean shirt and black jeans, put his black leather jacket over a chair, ready to slip into when they were about to leave. He now paced the kitchen wondering what took April and Belle so long. Was Belle so upset April couldn't get her to calm down? Or were they engaged in some deep meaningful conversation? About classmates and fitting in and…

He was glad April was taking the heat for him but at the same time he felt like a failure for not knowing how to do this himself. He had always felt quite competent in his role as single father because he loved his daughter, was there for her, gave her priority over work and anything else in his life. But as she grew up, he had realized that there were subjects girls just didn't like talking about with their fathers. And he had wondered how he was going to tackle that. Sure, he had a very kind-hearted elderly receptionist who drank a cup of tea with Belle every now and then, but he didn't have the impression they were close. It wasn't about finding some female, any female, who could get through to his daughter. It had to be someone Belle connected with, someone she could feel safe with and confide in.

He heard laughter and turned around. Belle came into the kitchen. She wore the dark pants-white blouse combo he had so adamantly supported, but with a sleeveless vest that glittered. The real shine however came from gorgeous sparkling earrings. With her hair up in a way he had never seen before the effect was…spectacular.

"You look so beautiful," he said and went over to give her a hug.

Belle beamed. "April helped me figure

out how to be me and look festive at the same time."

"That's good," he said and let go of her, turning to look at April. She wore a fluffy sweater with a large collar, in a cognac color that brought out the strawberry blond tints of her shoulder-length hair. It also strengthened the golden shine on her eyelids from a light dusting of shimmery makeup. Dark brown pants and ankle boots completed the ensemble. It was simple but effective.

"You look great," he said.

She smiled. "So do you."

Belle reached for the leather jacket he had put on the chair. "We have to be going. Or we will be later than everybody else."

"Yes, ma'am." Matt slipped into his jacket and turned to get his car keys. His idea to ask April to help Belle was working. He hadn't seen his daughter shine like that in ages.

Maybe never? She seemed suddenly confident and happy and...

How did April do that? She had a sort of touch with people... It was very special.

She was very special.

Knowing someone was sharing the responsibility for Belle's happiness with him was an unusual feeling, but it could be good.

APRIL STARED AT Matt's back. That leather jacket gave him an extra edge she liked. A spark of attraction she should squelch quickly if she wanted to have a good time here. Matt was an old friend, not a…potential partner?

She wondered for a moment if she could indulge in the fantasy, if only for tonight. After all, it wasn't the New Year yet. Why not let herself enjoy his company, this special night, the talking and maybe even dancing? Why not let herself drift on a warm feeling of being home again and it not being all that bad?

Then in the bleak light of morning she'd remember all the reasons why she and Matt weren't going to get together, ever. And she'd reaffirm her resolution.

Matt looked at her. "Are you ready to go? Don't you need a purse or something?"

"Yes, of course. One moment." She turned away, glad he couldn't see her confusion. It wasn't that he was handsome or her heart still responded to his nearness. She had known that all along. It was the realization that her rational mind would actually consider embracing a fantasy, even for one night, as if the two of them were... meant to be?

No. Definitely not. It had been possible in the past maybe, when she had worked for him at the hotel and she had grown close to him and Belle, and they had been almost like a little family. But these days... She had her promotion which meant she would hardly have any shore time anymore. And Matt didn't even see her as a woman. He had called her little Miss Sunshine, like she was still the Williams girl, the town tomboy.

She came back with her purse and gave Belle a reassuring nod. Step one had been conquered: the protective dad agreed to the outfit. Now Bobby had to notice Belle...

April felt a little jitter of nerves. Belle believed in her good judgment and if the guy in question didn't come over...

Matt opened the door of the SUV for April. He studied her expression as if he tried to tune in to her feelings. Did he notice she was nervous? Would he wonder why? After all, he probably didn't know about Bobby...

CHAPTER FOUR

MATT STOOD IN a corner of the party tent and emptied the glass of apple juice. With too many people crammed inside and the heaters turned on full force, it was getting impossibly hot. He had made the obligatory tour to say hi to town connections and friends, to compliment the mayor's wife as hostess of the party and to check that Belle wasn't being bothered by those girls who had pestered her earlier. Now he was wondering how he could prevent getting cooked in here.

A welcome cool breeze touched his face as someone entered through the flap nearby. This guest had obviously been outside for a while and Matt considered this a very good idea. With a bit of a guilty feeling as if he was skipping school he escaped into the fresh air of the December night. The crisp snow creaked under his footfalls.

The sky overhead was clear with a twinkle of stars. He recalled April had said it wasn't good for fireworks if it was cloudy. It seemed the weather had improved. Especially for her?

He grinned to himself. April was a force to be reckoned with. He could just picture her on a cruise ship dealing with difficult passengers or settling arguments among the staff. She was always calm and rational, wouldn't get caught up in emotions. She also had a sort of…endearing quality about her. People tended to like her and be willing to accommodate her.

There was no other way to explain how Belle who had been so upset about not having a fancy dress had suddenly felt totally fine in normal pants and a blouse. Of course the earrings had made all the difference.

Or the hairstyle?

He wasn't sure… He felt clueless in such matters. Which was why it was so good to have April around now to help Belle find her feet.

"Needed a bit of fresh air?" a voice asked close to him and he detected April huddled in the collar of her sweater, leaning against the trunk of a tree. She nodded upward. "It's a beautiful night."

"It sure is." He came to stand beside her. "I've always thought that out on the ocean where there is no artificial light you have to be able to see the Milky Way."

"Oh I bet, *if* I actually had a minute to stand at the railing at night and look up." April's tone was ironic. "I fear you have a much too romantic view of my job, Matt Carpenter."

Romantic… Was it romantic on a cruise ship? Would there be men seeing her as an attractive woman and trying to date her? Or maybe she was close to someone on the staff? He knew so little about her private life.

He shifted weight and watched his breath form a cloud in the chilly air. "I don't think I am much mistaken if I say you live for your work and there isn't much else in your life."

"Do you think that is wrong?" April's tone was teasing but her wide-open eyes seemed to ask an honest question, searching inside him for an honest answer.

"No," he said. *I'm just the same.* "I'm just stating a fact."

"Hmmm." She seemed dissatisfied with this noncommittal reply.

He glanced at her. On a festive night like this he didn't really want to dig into his home situation, but April's expectant expression coaxed him into it. "I sympathize, you know. I have the hotel and Belle and… I don't have time for much socializing either. Actually, that's fine with me. Nights like these…" He gestured over his shoulder at the overheated party tents from which a buzz of voices and laughter emanated. "Feel quite exhausting."

"Really?" Her eyes twinkled. "You have to make conversation for a single night, a few hours, and it's too much already?"

"No, that's not it. I could talk for hours to the right person. Here it's so…random. A word with our trusted shopkeeper, Mrs. Jenkins, here, two sentences about the past year with someone else there. It doesn't feel…very meaningful." He stamped his feet. "It doesn't have to be deep conversation all of the time of course, but all this small talk just…"

"I know. I slipped out myself because I was getting a headache from the heat. I feel better here." April smiled but with a hint of sadness. "I guess when you're traveling as much as I do, you sort of feel boxed in quickly when you're in one place."

Yes, that was April. Always chasing the horizon. She'd never be happy tied to a small town like Heartmont. That was why she had left.

He put his hands in the pockets of his jacket and stared into the darkness. "So how much leave do you have this time? Did you say six weeks?"

"Yeah. That's a lot. And it will be my last long leave too. I'm…getting promoted." Her eyes lit as she added with a hint of pride in her voice, "One-stripe officer."

"Really?" A warm feeling seeped through him that little April had managed to rise through the ranks. "Congratulations. You've worked so hard over the past few years, you really deserve it."

"Thanks. I guess now that I've got it, I realize how much it meant to me. The recognition that you're doing a good job.

Return on investment of time and energy and…"

"Yeah, I know what you mean. Some things in life are…important. Maybe more important than you yourself first thought." He waited a moment, breathing the cold air. He hadn't talked about this to anyone. Not even to Dad. It just didn't seem…necessary?

Or relevant? Who ever wondered how he felt? He was just doing what he had to do and it worked out and…

He said slowly, "You know I gave up football when I married Kennedy and we took over the hotel. It wasn't a difficult step at the time, because I loved her so much and there was our baby to consider." He hadn't exactly planned to marry at eighteen, but once Kennedy had told him she was pregnant, it had seemed the natural thing to do. He had loved her so much and also instantaneously felt protective of the life forming inside her. "People said that I was throwing away a big career, and my chance to make it as a football player. My scholarship as well. But it didn't feel like a giant sacrifice to me."

He searched for the right words to explain his innermost feelings. "It was so natural to come into the hotel business which I already knew inside and out, and at the same time build a home for my family… I loved football, sure, but I loved people more than any career I might have had. I thought Kennedy and I would grow old together. That we would always have each other, Belle, our family. Then Kennedy died and I was facing the world alone and…"

He frowned as he tried to formulate the change inside. "Over time I began to see that maybe football had meant more to me than I had ever acknowledged. I started coaching the little league team, purely as a volunteer without any qualifications… I loved it and I realized I needed much more knowledge. So I went to trainings and got some certificates and… Well, to make this long story short, I'm going to be taking an exam later in January to get an official license to become a trainer for a youth team."

"Wow, that's amazing." April beamed at him. She reached out and put her hand on his arm. "I'm so happy for you, Matt."

"It's a dream I can finally chase. Dad is

still fit enough to run the hotel with the help of staff and Belle is going to college after the summer so then I could, uh…apply to be a trainer for a team farther away maybe."

"You'd consider leaving Heartmont?" April asked. Her voice didn't betray whether she thought that was a good or a bad idea.

"If I get a nice offer… Who knows. It feels like I get a chance to start over. Now don't say this to Belle because I don't want her to feel like she was ever in my way, because she wasn't. I would have done anything for her. But she's older now, she's going to college and…it frees my hands."

"Wonderful." April looked him in the eye. "So we're both accepting a new challenge in the New Year. Moving on…"

There was an expression on her face he couldn't quite define. Was she pleased with these developments? Or also wistful, because life changed and… Well, sometimes it was hard to change with it.

"Wait a sec," he said. And he slipped back inside the party tent.

APRIL SHIVERED IN her sweater. It was too cold to stand around without a coat on. She had barely noticed when she had first come out, her cheeks hot and her head buzzing with the music, all the questions from well-meaning neighbors who hadn't seen her for so long. She appreciated that they cared enough to ask but when you had to talk, over and over, about life on a cruise ship, there came a moment where all you wanted to do was run away screaming. She had seen her mother on the other side of the room chatting with friends and Cade dancing with Lily. She had wanted to go over and talk to them, but the people who kept pulling her aside hadn't let her and maybe a party, where it was rather loud and chaotic, didn't lend itself to serious conversation anyway.

She had only meant to step out for a short breather, to pull herself together before facing another round of "how interesting that you live on a ship" conversation, but the unexpected heart-to-heart with Matt had kept her longer than intended. She had been grateful for his company as she had felt a little sentimental. Gina's sweet baby boy, the funny twins, the session selecting clothes with Belle, it had reminded her of dreams of old, of having children of her own, being settled somewhere with the handsome husband, the adorable children and the comfy home. As a girl she had always envisioned that home right here in Heartmont. Now she was thirty, single, newly promoted, oh yes, but still… Thinking of the sweet baby in her arms she had wondered for a few heartbeats if her hard-earned career would ever make her truly happy.

Then again, to have a baby she'd need a man she could commit to, wholeheartedly. And her heart was still taken. By the impossible option. Matt Carpenter, the only man she had ever been deeply in love with. Perhaps because she had idealized him. Did she even really know him? So much time had passed since she had left Heartmont to nurse her broken heart.

Besides, standing here now, the chill grazing her cheeks, she realized it was more impossible than ever. She had earned her stripe; Matt was chasing his dream of a return to football. Not as an active player, but as a coach. He'd be great at it, she just knew. He loved the sport and he was good with kids. Patient, encouraging. She had to be happy he had shared this news with her. Now she knew her own decision to let go of him was the right one. These few weeks here would be about separating herself, finally, from the dream of ever being special to Matt Carpenter. As she interacted with him, day by day, she needed to convince herself that they were just friends, and they'd never be any more than that. Maybe he'd even share with her that he was in love with someone else, or intended to look for a partner once he had his coaching license and was settled far away from Heartmont. Letting go of the fantasy of Matt and her together should feel like a liberation. Opening the door to new possibilities.

It shouldn't feel like loss. It shouldn't hurt like it did, now, deep inside.

"Here." Matt popped up again and offered her a glass. "I think we should toast. To new beginnings."

How appropriate. She had to swallow a moment before she clinked her glass against his. It was time to convince her silly heart to listen to reason. It was over. Had been for nine years. "To new beginnings."

Matt held her gaze as he added, "And to supportive friends."

Friends. Yes, that was what she and Matt had always been and would stay, forever. A good thing. Much needed in life.

She smiled and echoed, "To friends."

CHAPTER FIVE

"YOU SHOULD STOP by soon for dinner," Ma said as they hugged to say goodbye after the spectacular fireworks had brought the joy of the New Year among them. "I'll make your favorite stew." Her eyes held April's gaze for a moment as if to search for something in her expression. Perhaps the real reason why she had decided to check in with Matt, avoiding the ranch?

"Okay." April gave her a kiss on the cheek. "I'm happy to be home, Ma, even if I'm not staying with you. I just need...a bit more quiet during my leave."

Ma nodded. "I understand." She gestured in the direction of the ranch SUV in which Cade and Lily sat waiting for her. Judging by their joined silhouettes they were wishing each other a happy New Year all over. "These two lovebirds can be a bit much to stomach." She gave April another probing look. "Especially if you're not interested in romance."

April was glad her cheeks were already red from the cold. She wasn't sure if her mother had ever noticed her infatuation with Matt. Maybe, as mothers had an uncanny ability to understand what was going on inside their children, even if those children didn't want to share anything. "It's not that I'm not interested in romance. It's something that has to happen naturally. If you start chasing it, it can only lead to disappointment."

Ma wanted to say something—deny it maybe, or encourage her to keep trying?—but April stopped her with a hand gesture. "Ma, look at it this way—Cade's got a girl and that's more than you ever believed would happen. Admit it. He was so involved in work all the time you figured he'd never meet someone."

Ma smiled softly. "True. And if even a stubborn no-nonsense guy like Cade can fall so hard, there's also hope for you." She squeezed April's arm. "I'll be wishing for your happiness all year long."

April's eyes burned for a moment. She

could act tough and distant all she wanted, pretend she didn't need anyone special in her life, but when her mother said it like that… "Thanks, Ma." She hugged her again, burying her head a moment against her mother's shoulder.

A horn honked and they separated. April didn't know if it was Cade getting impatient or someone else. Maybe Matt even, waiting for her?

With a fiery flush in her face, she walked to his SUV. Belle hung in the back, scrolling on her phone. The expression on her face seemed forced neutral. Had something happened during the night? April felt a prick of guilt that she hadn't watched Belle more closely.

"Could we be social, Belle?" Matt asked as April clambered into the passenger seat and buckled up.

Without looking up from her phone, Belle said, "I got a ton of messages."

Matt hemmed. "Funny as you've just seen all your classmates in person."

"Not all of them," Belle retorted.

Uh-oh. Had Bobby not shown up? If he had missed glammed-up Belle, she had every reason to feel disappointed. Cheated out of this opportunity to impress him.

April tried to catch Belle's eye in the rearview mirror but the girl seemed absorbed by the words and images on her screen.

Matt said, "Don't bother. Once she's on that thing, there's no talking to her."

"You're just as bad," Belle said. "When you get to watching clips of football matches…" She rolled her eyes.

April suppressed a laugh.

Matt seemed to think it better not to engage. He turned the ignition on and maneuvered the SUV away from the other vehicles. People waved at him. "Fun night," April observed.

"And exhausting," Matt said suppressing a yawn. "I can't wait to fall into bed. You, Belle?"

"Hmmm," his daughter said noncommittally.

April rubbed her hands together. "The fireworks were stunning."

"You must have seen bigger ones in all the places where you've been." Matt glanced at her. "Sometimes I forget that you've been around the world and back a couple of times."

"I don't feel it's all that special. I mean, you get used to it." April leaned back in the seat, savoring the warmth of the car's heater. She looked out the window.

Matt seemed to take it as a sign she was tired and didn't want to talk because he turned on the radio. As it was well past midnight, it was nonstop music. Classic love songs like Matt's father had often played at the hotel. The words immediately transported April back to the days when she had sat at the reception desk, filling out the ledger or checking reservations on the computer and secretly waiting for when Matt would come in. Would he have a few minutes to chat with her? Would he suggest pizza for dinner? Would he ask her out to the playground with Belle? Her world had revolved around him and his little girl. The two people in the world she wanted to belong with.

Was that sad? Or had it been rather perfect? Until it had all ended with a bang. Because of a stubborn pony and…her being even more stubborn. Matt had told her not to ride Flame. He had called him skittish. April had thought Flame was just misunderstood. She could handle him, right?

April clenched her hands into fists. She had thought she could handle it. I Can Do It had become her motto, just because people often doubted that a girl like her could. She had wanted to show Matt how good she was and that he could leave things to her.

Then the accident had happened and...

Matt turned the radio off. The click broke the memories apart like bubbles and she surfaced to find they'd arrived at the hotel.

"Were you dozing off?" Matt asked.

His brown eyes were concerned, as if he registered her sad mood. But he didn't understand any of her feelings, never had. She had to keep that in mind. They weren't close. They had never been, only in her fantasies. It was time to wake up and see reality.

"Sort of." She stretched. "I'd better get into bed, or I'll fall over while brushing my teeth."

She got out and walked to the entry door. Belle followed hurriedly. She still had her phone in her hand but hissed to April, "I need to talk to you. Dad can't know. I'll sneak into your room in ten minutes."

April didn't have time to agree or object because Belle had already vanished inside. April's heart beat fast. Was Belle mad at her for giving her the wrong advice? Had Bobby not come? Had he not noticed her? Or worse, had he come over and had the encounter gone wrong? What could she say to a sad girl whose heart was breaking?

For a moment she had the overwhelming feeling that she couldn't deal with this. Not on top of her own sadness over Matt, the past, the incident with Flame and the tension with her family, all the bittersweet memories attached to being back here and not fitting in anymore.

But she had to shape up and be professional about it. Snap back to her persona on the ship. *I can solve anything a passenger comes up with. Because that is what I do. And what I do well. I can do it.*

In the hall Matt asked, "Did you have a good time? I mean… Maybe it was a bit much on top of having traveled here today…"

"Yesterday," April corrected with a grimace. "No, I had fun. But I'm bushed now. Good night."

"Sleep in and I'll cook a big breakfast when you're ready, okay?"

"Sure, thanks." April went to her bedroom and sank on the edge of the bed to zip open her ankle boots. She felt a sharp stab of regret that she hadn't tried to stretch the moments with Matt. He had looked as if he wanted to chat more. Why had she not suggested a cup of tea before bed? Anything to have time with him?

Because, she corrected herself, *I am trying to loosen my bond with him, not strengthen it. It's January first and the resolution is to fall out of love with him. Stick with the plan.*

There was a very soft sound at the door and Belle slipped in. She rushed over and said, "You can never guess what happened."

April looked up at her. All the indifference during the car ride was washed away from Belle's face and she looked incredibly excited. And happy.

April's own heart leapt. She scooted to the edge of the bed. "Did you see him?"

"Yes!"

"Did you talk?"

Belle nodded fervently. Her eyes sparkled and she clasped her hands together. "He said he likes me."

She waited a few moments and added, "Like really likes me, you know."

"I see." April's heart beat fast as if she was seeing the scene unfold. "Did he ask you out or something? You're beaming all over."

"We…" Belle sucked in breath and then whispered, "Kissed."

April stared at the bubbling joy in Belle's eyes, the dreamy smile around her lips, and for a moment she wished she herself felt that way. That Matt had kissed her while they had been outside, away from the rest. That instead of speaking of friends he had talked about being in love and had leaned over to softly press his lips to hers. How good would it have been to fall into his arms, to lose herself in the certainty that all was as it should be now. They had always been meant to be together.

But he hadn't kissed her. He hadn't suggested anything close to romantic feelings for her and she shouldn't be thinking these thoughts.

Most of all, Belle was waiting for a response.

"That's fantastic." April rose and hugged Belle. "I'm so happy for you."

"He said he came to the library a few times to see me but he didn't know what to say. And every time he was there and didn't say anything, I thought he didn't even notice me. I felt so silly for even thinking he could like me." Belle laughed. "Bizarre, huh? How both of us thought we shouldn't say anything and were tiptoeing around each other. But now he kissed me and… everything is alright." She clasped her hands to her chest and sighed deeply. "I can't believe it."

"Did he like…ask if you wanted to be his girlfriend?" April probed gently.

"No, but we didn't really have much time because someone was coming and… I guess he will message me?" Belle shrugged. "Whatever. It's alright now. He feels the same way." She walked around the room, gesturing about her. "Can you imagine he was interested in me too, all that time, and I never knew? It's just…unbelievable. I'm soooo happy."

"You deserve it. And see, you don't need a fancy dress to make it happen either. You don't need a ton of makeup if you don't want it. Just trust in your own gut feelings—be yourself."

"Yeah, thanks, April." Belle rushed over and hugged her again. "I thought you should be the first to know. The, uh…" She bit her lip a moment. "Only one to know. I don't want Dad to find out."

April's back stiffened. She was happy for Belle, but it wasn't her intention to be dishonest with Matt. To keep things from him. Important things. At least, she thought that his daughter being in love and dating was pretty important. And chances were that in a small town like Heartmont, he'd find out soon enough.

If Belle kept it from him now, there would be trouble down the line.

But instead of throwing this at Belle right away, April studied her sudden frown and asked softly, "Why not?"

"He won't like it. He'll say I'm too young. That I have to finish school first and then in college maybe I can date but…all my friends date and Bobby is super serious so…

it can't hurt. But Dad will just talk down about Bobby and we'll have a big fight and it will spoil everything. I'm happy now. I want to feel like this forever. Just don't tell him, okay?"

Although Belle's reasons made sense and April could easily see Matt arguing with his daughter about the boy she was in love with, she felt a niggle of doubt in the back of her mind at Belle's chosen strategy of silence. Was this smart? The truth was bound to come out and Matt would be upset at both Belle and April if they kept things from him.

On the other hand April had told him while he drove her to the hotel from the airport, that if she managed to get close to Belle she wasn't going to share the girl's secrets with Matt. So he sort of knew her position.

Right?

"Were you only acting like you were bored, etcetera, in the car?" she asked.

Belle nodded wildly. "If I had let my feelings show, he would have been suspicious right off the bat. He has to think I didn't have a really good time or something. You see?"

April's tired brain hurt at the reverse psychology. "Belle, I don't know if... Can't you simply tell your father you're being friends with this really cute boy and seeing if there's more to it and..."

"He won't allow me to date—I'm telling you. Look, I just need some time to prepare him for it. I want to invite Bobby over, pretending it's for a school project, doing homework together or whatever and then Dad can see how nice he is and how much he cares for me and... It will pave the way for an announcement that we're... more than friends. Trust me—it will be much better that way."

"I guess you have a point there." April rubbed her face. This wasn't the time for a long discussion about the matter. She had to sleep on it first and then maybe she could talk to Belle again and explain how keeping things from her father wouldn't help her convince him that she was mature enough to date. "Let's try it that way."

"Perfect." Belle carefully took off the earrings and put them on April's nightstand. "Thanks for letting me borrow them. They really made me feel different. Confident. Because you had told me to be me."

"I'm glad for it. Now let me remove your makeup. I don't want you to jump into bed with makeup on—it's so bad for your skin."

April put makeup remover on a cotton pad while Belle sat down on a stool. Removing the makeup from that quiet upturned face, April felt a lump in her throat. The little girl she had told bedtime stories to was growing up so fast. She was in love; she had been kissed. It was so bittersweet. She felt tears behind her eyes. Couldn't she understand Matt when he figured his daughter was too young for this? Why he wanted to keep her small and close to him, always? April had been away so often, had missed so much of Belle's development from the seven-year-old she had said goodbye to, to the young lady sitting here tonight and still it hurt inside to know she had to let go. That there was a young man now vying for this girl's heart and that soon Belle would be following her own path in life.

As April threw away the dirty pad, Belle

looked at her. "I'm so glad you came here. It's not the same as emailing you." She jumped to her feet. "Thanks for everything. Good night."

And she softly left the room and drew the door closed.

CHAPTER SIX

WHEN APRIL AWOKE, it took her a while to recall where she was. She was used to sleeping through noises and she fully expected to hear the familiar sounds of the ship around her. But as she tuned in to something suspiciously like silence, her senses came to full alert. What was wrong? Why weren't they moving? Had they docked for the night?

No. There were sounds though. Like… a horse neighing and hoofbeats? On the ocean?

Her eyes flew open. She wasn't on her beloved ship. She was home in Heartmont. On the ranch. Cade would be up already milking the cows and…

No, she wasn't at the ranch either. She was at Matt's hotel. She had been to the New Year's Eve party with him and…he hadn't kissed her.

With a groan April turned over. Her throat

was so dry. She normally got up early, drank a glass of water straight out of bed and did exercises before breakfast. It was a strict regime and as soon as she deviated from it, her body protested. But she was on vacation now. She could cut herself some slack.

She sat up and her gaze fell to the bag of chocolate coated raisins beside her bed. Would she…? It felt kind of decadent to eat chocolate while still in bed, but it was a new year and she could do whatever she wanted. She reached for the bag and pulled it open, poured raisins into her hand. As she savored the creamy sweetness of the chocolate, she closed her eyes and promised herself she would enjoy her time here to the fullest. No complicated thoughts, just pure fun.

After another handful of sugary goodness, she dragged herself out of bed and into the shower. Once she had blow-dried her hair and dressed, she felt energized for the day. Hadn't Matt promised her a big breakfast?

She checked her appearance in the mirror one more time, wondering briefly if the light blue sweater and jeans were a bit too casual. On the ship her wardrobe choices were limited and even when she went to shore she kept in mind that passengers might see her and it was good to exude professionalism. As she stood there watching her mirror image, it struck her for the first time ever that she was always considering other people's opinions rather than her own. And now that she had earned her uniform, she would be dressed in that, like…taking on the ship's identity? Was she turning into a machine more than a human being?

She shook her head. These thoughts were odd. She had worked hard, for years, to get this promotion. It was what she had always dreamed of. And a uniform didn't mean you lost your own personality. It was just a way of letting others see what your function on the ship was.

Still her doubts had unsettled her a little. She tried to chalk it up to fatigue. Tomorrow she'd feel different. Absolutely.

She left the room. There was a tantalizing scent of fried eggs in the air. She inhaled deeply and realized how hungry she was. With a smile she quietly walked to the kitchen and looked in. Matt was at the sink, pressing fresh orange juice. In a pan eggs sizzled and the oven dinged to indicate something was ready to be taken out.

She leaned her cheek against the door frame as she looked at his back, the way he moved graciously around the kitchen getting things ready. There was something about him that always gave her a comforting feeling inside. He was dependable, strong. Someone to come home to.

She forced herself to stand up straight. He was just a friend, remember? Nothing more.

"Good morning," she called. "Busy-busy?"

Matt turned and smiled at her. One dark curl fell over his forehead. "I'm almost done with breakfast for the guests. Then you can order."

His words hit her like a bucket of ice water. The guests. Of course. He hadn't been busy for her, but for others. This was his job, making sure people were satisfied with the service here. She was a guest too and he pampered her for that reason. Not because she meant anything special to him.

It was an unpleasant wake-up call, but

one she needed, bad. *Better keep it in mind.* "Could I have a glass of water? I'm used to hydrating as soon as I get out of bed and that's usually way earlier than this." She pointed at the clock on the wall which showed 10:15.

"Sure, there are glasses in the cupboard." Matt gestured over his shoulder. He carried a basket to the oven. "I need to take out these croissants. Do you want one? They're the best when still hot."

"Yes, please." April got herself a glass and filled it with water at the tap. She stood close to Matt and could smell his after-shave. She watched a moment as his strong tanned fingers grabbed each croissant off the plate and put them in a basket. He kept one separate for her. "Your fingers must be heat resistant if you can touch them when they come from the oven like that."

"Experience. I know how to do it so quickly I don't burn myself. Besides, I'm too lazy to get an oven mitt. I did have a blister one time to remind me I shouldn't be doing this." He winked at her. "But I never learn."

April leaned against the sink sipping her

water. She hated how her cheeks heated just because he winked at her. "What time did you get up?"

"Seven. Two of my guests were leaving and I checked them out and printed off some details about things to see and do in Boulder."

She tilted her head. "Weren't you tired after last night?"

"I knew they were leaving this morning so I should have stayed home. But I didn't want to. I had fun." He smiled at her again.

April clenched the cool glass. She had so told herself that she was going to see Matt in a friends-only light but it wasn't really working. She loved his dimples. "I didn't see you dance."

"I'm not a big dancer. Besides, it was too crowded in there. You're only bumping into other couples. It's painful." He had put her croissant on a plate and placed it on the kitchen island with butter and jam. "You start eating—I need to get these…" he held up the other croissants in their basket, "…to the guests. I turned what used to be the breakfast room into two more hotel rooms, so these days they get fresh breakfast supplies served to their individual rooms. It's more work, but two more rooms also mean more earnings."

"I see. You're expanding."

"I guess—eight rooms is the max for now. I mean, we're not fully booked year round so there are quieter times but in summer I'm on my feet from dawn to dusk. Caring for the horses, doing excursions with guests. I love it but I don't want the business to get too big for me to handle, you know?"

"Hmmm." April watched how the butter she had spread on the croissant melted and then she added strawberry jam. "How many horses do you have?"

"Six. And one retired pony to keep them company."

April gripped her knife tighter as she cut the croissant into bites.

Matt said softly, "I hope you don't mind that I kept Flame, April. I know your brother wanted me to sell him after he threw you off and you were injured, but I just couldn't get myself to do it. Flame wasn't vicious. He never meant to hurt you. He just misunderstood."

"No." April looked up at Matt. "It was

my fault. I rode him when you had told me not to."

"Not because I didn't trust you." Matt walked two steps closer to the kitchen island. "I knew you were good with horses. But Flame was different. I suspected he had been through some traumatic experience that made him shy away at the most unexpected moments. I thought he needed more time to adjust."

"And I thought a little love and attention could cure him of his bad moods." April smiled sadly. "I meant well."

"I know you did. That's why I felt so bad about what happened. I…" Matt looked as if he wanted to say much more but then he glanced at the croissants in the basket and said, "My guests are waiting for their breakfast." He picked up another basket that stood ready at the door with bottles of freshly pressed juice and fruit.

April sat in the empty kitchen. Was she saved by the bell? Or was it a letdown that he hadn't continued? She had never been able to figure out why Matt had decided to fire her even though she had wanted to stay on. He had explained to her at the time that it was wrong to keep her working for him when her family didn't support it. But that was nonsense. She had been twenty-one, not thirteen. It wasn't like Cade could decide her life for her. Back then or now.

She shook her head at the fierceness of her own response. It didn't matter anymore.

"Good morning!" Belle breezed in, all smiles. She wore a pink cardigan with stone-washed jeans and black boots. "Once you're done with breakfast, I want to go into town to show you the library where I volunteer. It's closed for the holiday but I've got a key and we can look around without anyone interrupting. I want to show you what I do there and…" She fell silent and added, almost shyly, "If you want to get a tour of the building."

"Sure. I only had those photos you sent earlier. It will be great to see where you work, in person."

Belle nodded and poured herself some leftover orange juice. "Is Dad busy again?" She glanced out the window as if she expected to see him out there. "He is a real workaholic, you know. If it isn't the hotel he's busy with the football team he trains."

She stopped herself and looked at April. "Did he tell you about his plans?"

April was confused a moment as Matt had said no one knew yet. But of course he had meant people outside his family circle, people other than his dad and Belle.

Still she queried carefully. "What plans exactly?"

"To become a football coach. He puts a lot of time into getting certificates and... studying for his license. I guess it's kind of weird to see your father worry about an exam. He thinks he might not make it."

"Why wouldn't he?" April asked. "I'm sure he tries hard to master the material."

"Sure, but... Dad is more the active type. He can explain field play like no other when he's with the kids in the field. But he's not into all the paperwork as he calls it. There is a lot of extra stuff that comes into it. Safety regulations, social skills. Psychology. He sits at night studying and I hear him moan."

April laughed. "Really?"

"Yeah. It's super awkward." Belle ambled over. "Do you want more breakfast?

I can get you yogurt with granola if you like."

"That would be fab."

"I'll make you something I really love. You like apricots, right?"

"I eat about anything." April leaned her elbow on the kitchen island and supported her chin in her hand. "It makes it so much easier when you travel a lot."

"I like trying new recipes." Belle produced fresh apricots and sliced them, removing the stones. "Here at home, that is. I don't know if I could travel like you do. I usually need time to adjust to a new place and sort of find my way around it. Sometimes I wish I was more adventurous and just threw myself into things."

"I can tell you it doesn't always work out well. Maybe you're better off looking before you leap." April played with the cuff of her sweater.

"Hello, sweetheart." Matt came in and kissed his daughter on the cheek. "Ah, you're whipping up your favorite breakfast?"

"For both me and April. She wants to try it. I can never get you to eat it."

"I don't like nuts and seeds." Matt made

an evasive gesture. "I stick with a huge bowl of oatmeal. Keeps me running all morning."

April had to admit his routine seemed to be working. Despite the short night, Matt looked fresh and ready to roar. He quickly washed up items from the sink, dried and put them away, while chatting to Belle about the guests who had left this morning. Belle was busy with glasses, yogurt and various bags of unidentified stuff. At last she turned and presented April with a glass full of layers. "That's the yogurt," April said, pointing, "and on top all the fresh apricot, but what's the rest?"

"Cereal, raisins, ground walnuts and almonds, chia seed…"

Matt grimaced behind Belle's back and April tried not to laugh. "That sounds great. I love the texture ground nuts give to a dessert or shake."

They both tucked into their breakfast while Matt cleared away the last of the used utensils and wiped a cloth across the sink. She'd love to have more quiet breakfasts like this, with two people around whom she felt so comfortable with.

Belle licked her spoon and said, "We're

off into town, Dad. I want to show April the library."

"Oh?" Matt held her gaze a moment as if waiting for more.

Belle flushed and turned away. "I'll get my coat. Can April drive your SUV?" She was already gone before Matt could reply.

He looked at April. "Are you up to an outing like that? It was pretty late last night."

"This morning," she corrected cheerfully. "Obviously, you have no idea about the hours we do on the ship. I'm often on my feet for twelve hours in a row. There's a lot to take care of and guests expect service around the clock. I guess people have misconceptions about cruise ship life. That it's almost like a vacation with a little bit of work attached."

"I never underestimated what you do." Matt held up both hands, as if warding her off. "But you are on leave now. You should be enjoying yourself."

"I'd love to see the library." April put her glass on the sink. "I never mind spending time with Belle, Matt. She's special to me."

He held her gaze and for a moment April wondered what would happen if she added, "And you are special to me too." If she reached out and put her hand against his cheek and watched to see if the look in his eyes would change. If she saw that he wanted her to touch him and lean in and… kiss him.

But what if he looked startled? Or if he actually pulled away from her and said: "Look, April, I'm sorry but that's not how I feel about you."

It would be so embarrassing she could never face him again. She had to keep things purely friend-like. For her entire stay here.

It suddenly seemed quite difficult.

"Ready to go." Belle reappeared in a deep purple coat, a black backpack in her hand.

April said, "I'll quickly grab my things." Her heart was hammering and she couldn't fully concentrate. Why was she constantly thinking about kissing Matt? She had promised herself she was going to say goodbye to those wishful thoughts about a relationship with him.

MATT WATCHED FROM the window as Belle and April got into his SUV. He tried to see something in April's posture but he didn't even know what he was looking for. Ever since last night there seemed to be…something different about her.

Or was there something different about him? He felt nervous, uncertain, on edge. Could it be about the exam? But it was still seventeen days until he had to take it. If he was going to have jelly knees all that time, he'd be a nervous wreck when he had to actually take the test.

He shook his head but he couldn't force himself away from the window. Seeing those two drive off for a cozy trip into town, he almost wished he had invited himself to come along. It was strange because it was counterproductive to his plan of letting April build a bond with Belle. But somehow he also wanted to be a part of it. Not for Belle's sake but for his own.

He couldn't deny he enjoyed April's company. She was still as down to earth, kind and funny as she had been years ago. Traveling the world and getting promoted hadn't changed her at all. But he shouldn't forget one thing that had changed. She was no longer a hometown girl, but a wanderer who never stayed in one place long. She had to feel like she had outgrown this place. The small-town mentality, the interest people had in their neighbors' lives. He considered it a kindness, but it could also feel like curiosity or even worse, meddling. April was fiercely independent. She didn't need anyone. She didn't need…

Him?

Why would he even want her to need him?

Still there had been something in her eyes as they had talked about Flame. About the past, the incident that had ended her job here at the hotel.

He couldn't help the feeling of panic that went through him when he recalled the day that he had found Flame's stable empty and he had realized April had taken him out for a ride. But that panic had been nothing compared to the emotions rushing through him when the pony had returned, alone, with the saddle half hanging from his back and no April. Something had happened. She could be hurt.

Matt closed his eyes a moment. He didn't want to remember, but his mind had other plans. His hands clenched into fists as he relived the anxiety he'd felt when he set out on his own stallion to look for April. How he had blamed himself, before he had even known what had happened. If April was injured, it would be his fault. He hadn't even wanted to think of her being...

Dead.

He snapped his eyes open. Yes. His deepest fear had been to find her lifeless on the ground, her neck broken after the pony had bucked and thrown her. Anger had fought with despair as he had looked for her. Anger because she hadn't listened when he had warned her that Flame couldn't be trusted. She had felt sorry for the animal. But emotions were dangerous and led people astray. Because she had believed he was condemning the pony, calling him unreliable, while he was just fearful, she had been drawn to do the forbidden. To take him out for a ride and show she could get him to trust her. April could do everything by herself, right?

Even now he felt the anger pulsating in his veins. Back then fear had wrung his throat shut. Fear that her mistake had cost her dearly. That he would have to call her mother and tell her April was dead. Like he had called Kennedy's family after the plane crash. "Kennedy won't be coming." She was on her way home. She was going to see her parents for the first time in over a year, after they had immigrated to Canada. That was why she had wanted to go, despite the fact that Belle had flu and a high fever. Normally all three of them would have been on that flight. But Kennedy had decided it was better for Belle not to travel in her condition so Matt had stayed home to care for her. Kennedy had been so excited about seeing her folks.

Matt bit his lip. Kennedy had died in a terrible accident. It had torn his life apart. And that day when he had looked for April he had feared that death had again pounced. That it was laughing at him as it stole his joy away, with an ice cold hand.

The moment he had seen her, lying on the ground, he had been so sure she was gone. But once he had dismounted and staggered to her on weak legs, once he had knelt beside her and reached out a clammy hand to touch her cheek, he had felt she was warm. He had seen her eyelids flutter. He had realized she was still breathing. She had opened her eyes and whispered his name. He had never in his entire life felt so relieved.

And so ready to shake her and tell her how scared she had made him. But he had told her to lie still until he had called a doctor to check she didn't have a spine or neck injury. He had busied himself with practical things to do for her, to drown out the emotion. The relief and the happiness and…

Matt turned away from the window abruptly. He had been worried about April because she had been working for him and had almost been hurt badly by one of his animals. He had been worried that her family would blame him, that it would be bad for his reputation in the region. Bad for business and all that. Nothing more.

Nothing personal.

But although he told himself that, as he had often done before, deep down inside he knew it wasn't the full truth. There had been more to it. There had been that weird echo of pain from the time when he had lost Kennedy, and the understanding, instinctively, that he had to shy away from April like a wild animal shies away from a bush fire. He had known he was better off keeping his distance, letting her go. Despite her tears and her apologies and her plea to keep her on at the hotel, he had told her to leave, find something else to do. Because of Cade Williams's urging, but also because…it had felt smart. Safe.

A cynical little laugh welled up inside him. He had probably been right about that. April's presence had a way of upsetting the balance, of making the quiet routine of his life go out the window. Things were different when she was around. He kind of liked that and that was why he had asked her to concern herself with Belle. He had thought it was a good idea to have those two spend time together.

He wasn't sure now what he thought. Last night Belle had first looked happy, then she had sulked on the way home. This morning she was cheerful again. He didn't understand any of it. Was it normal in teenage girls? Could April get closer to her? Would that help?

And what about himself? Should he spend

more time with April to figure out how he felt about her? Why there was this connection between them that felt so real again even if she had been away for years?

Or was it better to just ignore it? It made no sense to want anything with April this time around since they were both headed away from Heartmont. She'd be on her cruise ship again, newly promoted; he'd be pursuing his coaching dreams…

It had all looked so perfect up until now. He rubbed his neck. He so wanted his life to be clear, straightforward and neatly aligned. But right now it felt like one giant emotional tangle and he didn't know how to ever straighten it out.

CHAPTER SEVEN

"SO THAT IS the main entrance," Belle said, gesturing at the large glass-panel door leading into the building that had been the library when April was a child. She had often gone there to borrow books about horses and ponies, about the ocean and the jungle. She had rarely read fiction. The librarian, Mrs. Harris, had tried to interest her in books about girls who went to pony camp but April preferred to make up her own stories in which she was always, blissfully, alone. She didn't need the complications of friendships.

Standing here looking at the library, she wondered for a moment if she had always had that loner attitude. Apparently. Maybe that explained why she was still single? It took her forever to assess if she could trust people.

"Are you coming?" Belle asked.

"Yes." April flashed an apologetic smile. "I was just thinking how little has changed since I went to the library as a girl."

"Inside it has changed a lot." Belle grinned. "I helped grow the catalogue. We have a lot more Young Adult books now. But I also asked patrons what they like and we bought more cookbooks and crafting books. Come on—I'll show you."

They rounded the building to the back. Belle pulled a key chain from her backpack and looked for the right key. She pushed it into the lock which opened with a click. The small wooden door creaked as it swung open. They came into a narrow corridor. "We can hang our coats here." Belle gestured at the pegs on the wall. "There is a small kitchen area where we make coffee, tea and hot chocolate."

She walked ahead of April. "That's the door into the actual library." She put her hand on the knob and took a deep breath. Then she flung it open and said, "Ta-da."

April went inside. Normally she would have come through the other door of course and she had never entered this way, but still she immediately saw the differences.

The large reception desk had made way for more bookcases. There was even a cozy red couch in the corner where people could sit and read and have a chat. A single sleek computer served to check the catalogue.

Belle followed her gaze and said, "Most people check out books on their phone or tablet. And we're always here to help people who don't have a lot of digital skills. I really love giving book recommendations."

April took in all the loving touches: the book-shaped announcement board with flyers of local activities, the corner for the youngest patrons with pillows and teddies, posters on the wall. Care and attention had gone into every square inch of this space that breathed book love. She said, "You did an amazing job. How many volunteers are there?"

"Ten. And there is our paid librarian."

"I assume it isn't Mrs. Harris anymore?"

"No, she retired two years ago. It's Mrs. King now. She organizes a lot of things. A book fair, literary nights… Not everyone thinks it's necessary." Belle shrugged. "The mayor wants to cut back funding for the library, but we talked to his wife and she is working on him to forget about his plans." Belle sighed. "It's because of the storm that hit last July, you know. There was so much damage that had to be repaired. The town council has to make hard choices where to invest the funds."

April nodded. "I guess you could do fundraising."

Belle grimaced. "We've had so many fundraising events already. To cover all the storm damages. People aren't in for another event." She stood beside the Christmas tree in the far corner and pulled at a red card that was attached to one of its branches. "I guess we have to get rid of this too. It's January after all. Too bad for the wishes."

"What wishes?" April asked.

"These wishes." Belle tapped the red card with a finger. "We asked patrons to take a card, fill out their wish for Santa and hang it in the tree. Then the town council chose a wish to fulfill. I just feel a bit sorry for all those people whose wishes weren't chosen."

She turned a card toward her and read, "'Dear Santa, I wish for a puppy to take care of. I have no brothers and sisters to play with so I want to play with the dog.

Joey.'" She gave April a sad little smile. "I know what it's like to be an only child. I was never unhappy—I had Grandpa and Dad—but…you do have to always play by yourself or go over to friends. You don't have someone near, in the next room, to play with and cuddle."

"Do you know Joey?" April asked.

"Yes, he comes in here a lot. He likes books about pirates. He wants to find his own gold treasure. But his parents will never let him have a dog. They run the antique store and live over it. They won't want a live animal anywhere near their precious items."

"Hmmm. But couldn't we think of a way for Joey to have a dog without it having to live in his house? A dog he can care for away from home? Like a dog to walk?"

"Maybe." Belle tilted her head. "What are you thinking?"

"That those wishes…" April came over to the tree and gestured across all the cards hanging from it. "Can still come true. I have a six week leave. I have nothing to do. We could set about fulfilling wishes."

She felt energized at the idea of helping other people have a bit of happiness in their lives after all the stress caused by the summer storm and the subsequent repairs. It was also a good excuse for spending lots of time with Belle and keeping an eye on things between her and Bobby. Time also to chat and find out why she had been distant with Matt lately.

Or had that just been caused by her insecurity about Bobby's feelings and would it be resolved now? Anyway, to stay in touch with Belle in a natural way she needed some project and this presented itself readily.

"What a great idea," Belle said. She reached up to untie a card. "Let's take them all down and see what they say."

"I guess if the wishes are expensive, we will have to say no. But we can make connections." April leaned down to look at a card on a low branch. "Here someone is saying she'd wish she could have dinner some time at the steak house. Maybe the steak house owner can invite her over for a free dinner in exchange for something else?" She untied the card and put it on a stool nearby. "And this one…" She reached up. "Is about wanting new flower baskets for her porch. With a little help from the local garden centre we can certainly arrange that."

April's mind was buzzing with ideas as she gathered the cards and put them in stacks: material wishes, wishes for friendship or social activities… Everyone had been pretty reasonable, not asking for a jackpot win or a luxury cruise. These were normal everyday wishes for a special treat, for company or improvements for the entire community. Her heart warmed as she thought of ways she might be able to do something for the people in this small town she had grown up in. Maybe Heartmont wasn't where she lived anymore, but it would always have a piece of her heart.

She noticed from the corner of her eye that Belle was on her phone, then turned back to the task of getting all the cards off the tree and making an inventory of wishes and a plan for…

"No!" Belle cried and she dropped her phone to the floor.

April looked at her and rushed over. "What's wrong?"

Belle held her hands to her face. "No, it's not true. It's not."

"What is wrong?"

"A really mean message. It…" Belle burst into tears.

April instinctively picked up the phone. The screen had gone black. The glass didn't seem to be damaged. She wasn't sure what to do next, but Belle said in a small voice, "Look for yourself."

April swiped to open. A text filled the screen. A photo of Belle and a boy kissing. The text underneath read: Congratulations, Bobby, you kissed the ice queen and won the bet. Your new smartphone will be delivered to your house tomorrow.

April blinked. "What is this?"

"They made a bet. Because I don't look at boys much and… They call me the ice queen. They made a bet that whoever could get a kiss from me…would get a new smartphone. And Bobby…" She swallowed hard.

April's heart sank. She clenched the phone. "No, you're reading that wrong."

Belle looked at her with blotched cheeks, eyes full of tears. "Then how do you read it?"

April looked at the photo, the text. Her

brain scrambled to come up with something, anything, to wipe the hurt away from Belle's face. But she knew she couldn't. There was no other way to interpret it...

"They're lying." She said it through clenched teeth. "They are lying to drive you two apart. There is no such bet and he's not getting a phone. Don't believe a word of it."

Belle bit her lip. "They do call me the ice queen. So why wouldn't there be a bet?"

"Look, Belle, anyone could have taken a photo of you two and then..."

"The photo is the proof. It isn't random." Belle's voice screeched. "He kissed me so some other guy could snap a photo and he'd have proof. That's why he never asked me to be his girlfriend. That was not what he wanted. He only wanted a new phone."

April squeezed her shoulder. "You don't know that."

"And now they have sent this photo to everyone in class. I can never show my face again..." Belle broke off and stared at her. "Quick. We have to get away from here. Take me home so I can hide. This is the worst."

April slipped the phone in her own pocket

and took Belle by the shoulders. "Calm down. You don't know what happened and…"

"I want to get away from here." Belle pulled free and ran for the exit.

April hesitated a moment but there was no talking sense into her now. She quickly snatched the Christmas tree wishes and raced after the distraught girl.

MATT WAS ON the porch repairing a creaking floorboard when the SUV came into the yard. He looked at his watch, thinking they hadn't stayed away as long as he had expected. He had figured Belle would do a full tour of the library and then take April to lunch at Belle's favorite place and then… But they were back already.

The door opened and Belle came out. Her face was red. She rushed to the house, ignoring him as he said hello. She ran inside. Had her eyes looked a little red? Had she been…crying?

Matt shot to his feet and wanted to go after his daughter, but April's voice said, "Don't."

Matt whirled to her. "Why not? What happened?"

"I'll talk to her."

"No, I want to talk to her." Matt's heart-beat drummed under his breastbone. What had happened? Why had Belle cried? Had she told April something terrible?

"Now is not the time," April said.

"She's my daughter." *And no way you're going to keep me out of this.* He wanted to go inside anyway, but April grabbed his arm. There was surprising strength in her grip. "Please don't."

He looked into her eyes. He saw deter-mination there, to fight him on this issue, but also a plea for understanding. He took a deep breath. Everything inside him screamed that he had to get to his daugh-ter even if he had to break down her bed-room door to reach her, but something in April's expression got through to his pan-icking brain. She meant what she said. It was important.

He asked breathlessly, "What happened?"

"She got a message on her phone that upset her and she wanted to leave town in a hurry."

Matt exhaled. "Those girls again. Those bullies." He flexed his hands. His anger deflated into a sense of frustration and helplessness. He so hated to feel this way. "There is nothing I can do about them. Belle doesn't want me to talk to their parents or inform the school."

"She is sixteen, Matt, not six. You can't solve everything for her. Besides, if you talk to the parents, and they talk to the girls, those girls will feel caught out and angry and they will continue and probably do even worse."

"So you're saying I should just do nothing? My daughter comes home in tears and I just return to fixing my porch?"

"No, that's not what I'm saying. But you want to rush in and…" April's expression softened. "Put a kiss on her knee because she fell off the swing and hurt herself. But she's older now, Matt, and she hurts in different ways. It's no longer simple to solve her problems."

His sense of having failed kicked in full force. "They were never simple to solve, April. How can you tell a little girl that her mother is not coming back? That she fell from the sky in an airplane and…" He closed his eyes a moment. "I miss Kennedy. She would have known what to do now."

APRIL STARED AT Matt's tense features. Her heart ached for him and she wanted to reach out and touch him and tell him it would be alright. But he was just saying he missed the wife he had lost. She would have known what to do. Of course. Because Kennedy had always known what to do. Judging by the stories Matt had told her back then, Kennedy had been that ideal woman, the perfect mother and…

What was April even doing here? Matt wanted to help Belle himself but then he also didn't know what he was doing so…

What a mess.

Matt opened his eyes and looked at her. He exhaled in a long sad sigh. "I just don't know, April. I can fix this porch. I can fix so many things in my life. But I can't fix the fact that my daughter grew up in an all male household and… I guess I can't be everything she needs. And it gnaws at me."

"It may be the truth, Matt, but it's not your fault. We can't be things we are not." *I can't be Kennedy. I can't even try to replace*

Kennedy. I have to accept that. "We all have our strengths and weaknesses. That's why we need each other. To fill in the gaps."

"Then help me." Matt stared at her with pleading eyes. "Help me reach my daughter who won't talk to me anymore. Those school bullies…" He fisted his hands again. "I tell Belle to ignore them, to rise above it. But deep down inside I wish that those bullies could for once feel the same anguish, the emotional torment, that they unleash on my daughter."

April's eyes burned. She had just seen the effect of that one message. How Belle had changed from a happy self-confident young woman into a crying mess. How she had believed it was her own fault even, in some inexplicably crooked way. It had also made April angry. Angry and determined.

She still had her hand on Matt's arm. She now changed her grip from restraining to supportive. "Look, we can help her. But we have to allow her space. Yes, they are hurting her, but you and I both know that in life you're bound to get hurt. People make promises and they don't keep them. They betray your trust. They hurt your feelings.

They sometimes even outright break your heart. Belle will experience all those things sooner or later even if you don't want her to. Even if you want to hold her in your arms and make sure she never ever has a reason to cry."

Her voice quivered a moment. "You want to protect her, Matt, but you can't. Belle will have to have her own experiences, happy and sad. You can only be a safe haven for her, so she knows she can come to you and tell you everything."

"But she doesn't know that." Matt sounded hoarse. "She avoids me. She thinks she can't trust me."

"That is not what she thinks." April shook her head. "Matt, try to understand how hard this is for her. She is incredibly disappointed and then she comes to you and…what would you say? 'I told you not to care about what those girls say' or 'I told you not to…' You'd mean well but… I remember how it was when I was sixteen and I had problems. Cade was so protective and he did it out of love, but I just wanted him to…let me go and determine my own path in life. By trying to interfere all the time, he alienated me. I still find it hard to be close with him. While I do want to… I love my brother, Matt. Honestly. But so much happened." She patted his arm. "Please, please don't lose your daughter now. You two, you are special."

There were tears in Matt's eyes and April's heart squeezed. She wanted to throw her arms around him and hug him and tell him it would be okay. That she was there for him and would always be.

Always? But hadn't she decided she had to get over him and move on? What was this?

Just feelings running high over Belle. They were what connected Matt and her. His daughter. Nothing personal. Nothing… romantic?

Matt took a deep breath. "I'll try to be the best father to her that I can. But I don't know how to wipe her hurt away. All I want to do is blow away the tears on her face and make her laugh again. That's what I used to do when she was just a little girl."

April nodded. She couldn't speak now or she'd cry herself. She had often seen Matt with little Belle, picking her up when she had fallen off the swing and comforting her. Blowing her tears away and then kissing her better. Oh, those early happy carefree days... How far away did they seem now.

"Belle knows you love her," she managed to say. She swallowed hard. "She will confide in you again—I know that. But you have to let her struggle."

"I'm afraid." His voice was almost inaudible. "Afraid she's alone and desperate and she will make impulse decisions, irreparable mistakes. I need her to know that there is not a problem in the world we can't solve together." He grabbed April's hand. "I need you to make her see that. You understand? I told you yesterday and now you see it for yourself. Help her, April. Help me. Please."

April didn't need such pleas. This was exactly what she herself wanted. But how to achieve it? And Matt didn't even know the whole story. He thought the message had been about Belle's clothes or behavior, but this was much worse. It was a betrayal larger than life, crushing everything Belle had dreamed of. Breaking her very heart.

"I'll talk to her," she said. "I'll try my

very best to…" She fell silent not knowing what to promise him that wouldn't sound like an outright lie. "I'll go to her now." She stepped away from him and went inside.

MATT STOOD FEELING an enormous emptiness around him. His head spun and he didn't know what was up or down. He could only think: I'm losing my daughter. I'm losing my little girl. I can't lose her. Not her too.

Feeling so uncertain, so undone, brought back all the memories of losing Kennedy, of trying to fill the empty place she had left in their lives. It felt like he was that clumsy young father again who had no idea how to hush a crying four-year-old who kept asking for her mommy. April was so right. Some things you couldn't solve not matter how much you wanted to. He couldn't protect Belle against hurt. He couldn't.

He went to the stables and saddled his favorite horse. He had to be alone and think this over. Even if he already knew there was nothing he could come up with to get out of this quicksand. It was sucking him under and the more he struggled the faster it went.

APRIL HAD FILLED a glass with water and knocked on Belle's door. There was no reply at first, then a muffled, "Go away."

"It's me, April. Can I just come in for a moment?"

Silence. April hesitated. She didn't feel comfortable simply opening the door. Belle was entitled to her privacy and shouldn't feel like her room was being invaded or her decision not respected. At the same time April knew that sometimes the pain urged people to say no to things they did want or need. She had to find out if Belle needed her, now.

The door opened a crack and Belle looked out. "You talked to Dad. You told him everything."

It sounded half accusing, half desperate.

April opened her mouth for a retort, but Belle said, "You were outside for a long time. I know you talked."

"He immediately assumed it was those girls again. The bullies. He told me how powerless he feels to help you against them. He even wanted to go to their parents or to the school. But I talked him out of that. You don't want that, do you?"

Belle shook her head. She seemed a little relieved now. "So Dad doesn't know about... Bobby?" His name sounded strangled.

"No. I would never share that without your permission."

Belle nodded. She opened the door wider. "Come in then." Without waiting for April she walked to her bed and fell on it, face down. She hugged her pillow.

April closed the door and put the glass of water she'd brought on the side table. "I would never tell your father anything that you told me, unless you said it was okay. You understand that?"

Belle grunted.

April continued, "I can't claim I played a big part in your life these past years, as I was away so much, but... I did think of you often. I sent you the cards to let you know. I hope...you felt that."

Belle rolled on her back. "Why did he have to do this to me? Kiss me and then... For a phone. It feels so...pointless." She turned her head to April. "I would never accept a phone I had won in such a despicable manner. So I guess he's totally different from what I thought him to be. He only pretended to like books and stuff, to win me and have that phone. How weird is that. I can't really get it. I mean…" Belle put her hands under her head and stared at the ceiling. "I try to understand it. I thought that would help. To not feel so bad about it. So he wanted a phone and he couldn't get it from his folks, so he heard of this bet and then he told himself it was so easy, just kiss a girl and get a phone. Nothing hard about it." She looked at April again. "I guess a kiss means nothing to him."

"There are boys who feel that way," April confirmed.

Belle nodded. "And how do you know the difference?"

"The difference?"

"Yes, between boys who don't think a kiss is anything special and those who do." Belle's lips twitched as she fought tears. "Or aren't there any who think it's special?"

"Of course there are." April leaned over. "Don't you ever let some boy who's just not worth it ruin your idea of what a truly good man can be. They are out there."

"You haven't met one yet." Belle stared at her with damp lashes.

April looked down. "I met one but he got away."

"What happened? Did you ever kiss him? Were you together and did he leave you? I don't understand. You just said he was a good man... How could he be when he let you go?"

April smiled sadly. "I never told him how I felt. It was...complicated." She sat up straighter. "We're not talking about me now. But about you and Bobby. I feel we need a plan to work this out."

"A plan?" Belle echoed in confusion.

"Yes. We need to work out what truly happened before we jump to conclusions. Like who took this photograph? And did Bobby even know about it?"

"You think he might not have?" Belle scrambled to sit up. Hope shimmered in her eyes. "He didn't betray me?"

"I don't know that, Belle. But I feel like we should find out more before we write him off. You understand? You hoped he would notice you for a long time. You were so happy last night. Can all those dreams just go out the window?"

"No, you're right."

"Exactly. So I want to know more. And I think I know a way to find out. But I need your phone."

"Okay…" Belle scrunched up her face. "What are you going to do?"

"I can't tell you all the details yet. And you shouldn't get your hopes up that I can save your chances with Bobby. But I want to try."

Belle smiled. She reached out and hugged April. "You're the best. I can always count on you."

April was overwhelmed with tenderness as she held this mix of girl and woman in her arms. Someone so dear to her. Someone so precious she understood why Matt ached to protect her. She also wanted Belle to be happy, to see her laugh and dance.

She wanted Matt to be happy when he saw that. She needed to see that smile on his face and the warmth in his eyes and… She hugged the girl tightly and said, "Leave it all to me."

CHAPTER EIGHT

MATT DROVE HIS SUV into the yard of a neighboring ranch and got out. He felt hot under the collar with embarrassment that he was an hour late to pick up special feed for his horses. He had been riding around aimlessly trying to get a handle on his feelings about Belle, the past and…April. When she had stopped him on the porch, had touched his arm, something inside him had responded to her touch. Something more than just understanding when she said that he shouldn't crowd Belle. He had felt a connection between them beyond the common goal of wanting his daughter's happiness. Even if Belle hadn't needed a confidant, he would have wanted April to stay with him. Cook and eat with him, sit and talk with him. He wanted her around.

But he didn't want to feel that way, add even more emotions to the already explosive mix. He had tried to reason with himself that April was just a friend and he needed her in that capacity, more than ever. He shouldn't ruin the friendship by... wanting more?

He hadn't looked at his phone when it rang. The second time either. Only the third time had he answered and then been forced to mumble some excuse to explain his tardiness.

Hank Carruthers came over and shook his hand. "Glad you could make it anyway. I've got the bag ready. Shall I toss it in the back of the SUV?"

"Sure. Can I lend you a hand?"

Together they moved the heavy bag in the back. Hank said, "Let me know if you need more shortly. I have to order it especially and it can take a few weeks to come in."

"Will do."

Hank's wife, Marly, came from the barn, carrying their young son on her arm. She came over with a smile. "Hi, Matt."

"Hello." Matt leaned over to grab a small hand. "Hello there, little fellow. How are you today?"

"He's just taking his first steps," the

proud father said. Matt felt a little twinge inside. Those happy days when you could still carry a child on your arm, pick them up, comfort them and kiss away the tears. It was all so easy. He missed it. And if he started a new relationship, he might become a father again. Have that joy, the precious first months and years.

He blinked. What was this? He was the father of a beautiful daughter, who was getting ready to graduate next year and go to college. He wanted to become a football coach, have time to fulfill the dreams he had as a teen. His personal dreams which he hadn't had much room for earlier. He had no regrets but he did want the chance to try again and succeed this time. Not as player but as coach. Why would he suddenly allow himself to think about getting closer to April or about babies being cute? That made no sense at all.

Marly said, "Hold Dylan for me, Hank, I want to talk to Matt for a minute."

Hank seemed confused. "Uh, what?"

Marly shoved their son into his arms and gestured for Matt to follow her to the house. Once inside, she said, "I'm so sorry I have to tell you this, Matt, but I feel like you should know. I, uh…" She fidgeted with her hands. "Last night at the party I saw your daughter with a boy."

Red alerts began flashing in Matt's mind. Belle's attitude after the party, the tears later… Had some boy hurt her feelings? Told her she wasn't pretty enough or something else?

Marly said, "They were kissing." She avoided looking him in the eye. "Normally I wouldn't be such a snitch as to tell you but… I happened to see a message my niece got. She's in Belle's class. She was…laughing about it with a friend. It seems, uh… This boy kissed Belle as part of a bet and now he's won a new phone."

Matt blinked. "Sorry?" He had probably simply misunderstood. She couldn't actually be telling him that some oaf kissed his daughter merely to get his hands on a new phone?

Marly said, "I'm so sorry, Matt. I know how much you love Belle and this must be so hurtful. I wish I had known last night and I would have gone over to them and given that boy a piece of my mind."

"Leave that to me," Matt said grimly. "Who was it?"

"I think Belle should tell you that." Marly stepped back. "I don't want to have it on my conscience that you go over all hotheaded and…"

"I won't…" *Do anything drastic? Hmmm.* Matt said, "Thanks for telling me, Marly." He walked out the door. He was vaguely aware of Hank waving him goodbye with a sheepish expression. Poor man had no idea what bombshell his wife had just dropped. Women always knew more than…

Wait. What?

Matt stood with his hand on the door of the SUV. April had known. This morning when they had come back from town, with Belle in tears… April had known. Belle had to have shown her the message about the bet. Had to. She had known and…had not wanted him to know. That was why she had stopped him from following Belle inside. She had thought it was better if he stayed out of this.

How could she? Belle was his daughter. He had a right to know. A right to…

Matt got in his SUV. His pent-up frustration about this shameless wager refocused away from the nameless culprit to April who had known about the situation and had not told him. How could she simply decide that and…

He needed to talk to her. Urgently.

APRIL MOVED THE spatula in the spiced pork. Belle sat on the counter watching her. "It smells like it's going to be pretty hot. Are you sure that's the original recipe?"

"I learned how to make this in Costa Rica. They sell it a lot at street vendor booths. You'll love it. Even as a little girl you liked to try new foods. You weren't one of those kids who shies away from anything unfamiliar." April smiled at her. "You were different."

"Yeah. I feel like I'm always different. And it isn't good. I wish I could fit in. Be what the others want me to be." Belle banged with her heels into the counter. "I know I should be myself and all—I've heard it all before. But I just want to have close friends like the other girls and…be a part of everything. Sleepover parties and chats about boys and… I'm always an outsider."

"Hmmm." April put the lid on the pan to let it simmer a few more minutes. She checked that the wraps in the oven were almost ready. The salad was on the table. But would Matt be here? He had left and she wasn't sure what he was doing or when he'd be back. He was probably just working, taking care of a million things that a hotel required but she felt like he was avoiding her. Or was it just her own guilty conscience because she hadn't told him the reason for Belle's sadness? Matt was bound to find out sooner or later and he wouldn't understand why she had kept it back from him. Her heart beat faster just thinking of a confrontation about it. She fully supported her earlier decision but still… It would hurt if he blamed her, said things in anger.

She turned to Belle again. "I was always different as a child. I liked to be on my own. I explored the grass for insects and scoured the woods to find the nests of rare birds. I loved nature. I loved horse riding. I always imagined…that I would live on a big farm with animals and… I'd never have to see a single human."

"You wanted to be all alone? Didn't you love your parents, your brother and sister?"

"Oh I did, but… I just wanted to do my own thing. Determine when I got up and when I went to bed and what I called my chickens. You know that my brother, Cade, always laughed at the names I gave my chickens? And why? It was no skin off his back. But he always laughed at me." She shook her head, half mocking the indignation she had felt as a child. But she got serious as she continued, "I just wanted to be seen as someone who was entitled to her own opinions and choices. A person, not just a…part of something. Part of a family, part of a town. I guess going far away and being all by myself taught me to know who I am, what I want."

"On the cruise ship you're always with other people."

"Yes. But they're not family or friends. There is the other staff with whom you do form a bond, but more of a superficial one. And then there are the passengers whom you treat with respect and keep your distance. You are there to serve them. You're someone they barely notice. They want you to be friendly and efficient and that's about it. Nobody cares whether you like your work or you miss home. Maybe I'm exaggerating a bit but you get what I'm trying to say. Here in Heartmont I was always the little Williams girl. Everybody mothered me and felt entitled to an opinion about me. When I started on the cruise ship I was April Williams, the deckhand. I was a good deckhand or a bad one, based on the achievements I showed them. They didn't know me from before. They didn't have any preconceived notions about me. It was a completely fresh start. And I loved it."

April smiled at Belle. "I really needed that. Lots of people go away from home, they backpack or travel and they miss home. But I never experienced that. I was suddenly totally free and it was glorious."

"I think I would miss Dad. I would worry how he was doing. If he was working too hard. If he ever took time off. Slept in. Or did a fun movie night." Belle shrugged. "I organize those things and I think if I wasn't there he'd forget all about himself. He's always taking care of others."

April took a close look at the salad even if it was already perfect. "Didn't he ever feel the need to, uh…"

"Date or something?" Belle huffed. "Mrs. Jenkins from the mercantile tried to set him up with dates several times. But all he did was go to the diner or the cinema and then he found some excuse not to go on a second date. And there was this one woman whom he saw a few times, but she didn't like the hotel or me."

April looked at Belle who plucked at her jeans. "She told Dad that she wasn't about to throw away her life for a guy with a daughter and never-ending work."

"That doesn't sound like someone your father should get together with in the first place." April did feel a little smug for a moment and then berated herself for it. Matt was entitled to happiness and Belle had reason to agonize that he wasn't taking care of himself. Oh he looked in good shape but he was just working, working, working, never doing fun stuff and…

"Maybe we can do a movie night with the three of us," Belle said. "If you like?"

"Sure, why not? Oh, I hear your father's car." April's heart skipped a beat. Matt had obviously been angry at the people hurting his daughter and she hoped he would not show it too clearly to Belle. They needed to unwind a bit and forget about the photo until they knew more.

Matt came inside. He walked over to Belle and kissed her on the cheek. "Hey, sweetheart. How was your day?"

"Fine." Belle pointed at the stove. "We're trying a new recipe April picked up in Costa Rica. Prepare for an assault on your taste buds."

Matt nodded. "I see. Well, I guess after everything else that got assaulted today, my taste buds will now have their turn."

"How do you mean?" Belle asked. "Did something happen?" She scanned his appearance. "Did you fight with someone?"

April looked at Matt. His clothes weren't askew and although the wind had tousled his hair, he looked pretty normal to her.

Matt said, "I contemplated it. But I guess a sixteen-year-old boy is no match for me and I'd be in police custody by now. You would be hopelessly embarrassed so I will just have to think of another way to get even with him. In the movies I'd probably dump a ton of fish in his expensive sports car but in Heartmont the car would probably not cost as much as the fish I'd need."

Belle suppressed a laugh. Still her eyes were serious as she said, "So you know." She sounded resigned. "Who told you? Mrs. Jenkins? I knew it was just a matter of time until the whole town would know."

"It was Marly Carruthers. She saw you two last night."

Belle stared at the floor. April felt a little superfluous but didn't want to break the moment by trying to shuffle her way out of the kitchen.

"I guess," Matt said, "that I should congratulate my little girl that she's all grown-up now and falling in love…" His voice quavered. "But I just wish you hadn't found out so soon how painful being in love can be."

"Oh, Daddy…" Belle threw herself off the counter into Matt's arms. He hugged her tightly. Over Belle's head he looked at

April. She saw the pain in his eyes but she knew he had done the right thing tackling it this way. Not coming in fuming, not asking a hundred questions, but just letting Belle know he was there for her.

He was amazing.

Matt patted Belle's back. "Welcome to the club of the brokenhearted, little one. Now I know how grown-up you've really become."

Belle sobbed on his shoulder. "I wish it had been different, Daddy. Last night I thought…"

"I know, sweetheart. I know."

MATT HELD HIS daughter as closely as he could. His heart bled for her, but there was also a spark of joy that he had done this right. That he had reached out and found her again, in the darkness and the fog of his confusion. That he had managed to put aside his own emotions and find a way to her.

He saw April standing there smiling softly at him and her eyes told him that she also thought he had handled it right. That meant even more than his own conclusion. He could do this. Even if he didn't know how, he could do it.

And that April should be here now, being part of this precious moment, was just right. When he had driven home, he had blamed her for keeping the truth from him. But she had done so to prevent him from making a terrible mistake. This morning he could never have handled this the way he handled it now. The time away, and even being angry at her and wondering why she had done this, when she knew how much he cared, had prepared him for this moment. He had passed this test because of her influence. Because she seemed to know, instinctively, what people needed. She was amazing. And she belonged here.

The thought was brief and he didn't have time to attach meaning to it as Belle loosened herself and said, "We shouldn't forget about dinner."

"Right." Matt dangled his arms that suddenly felt empty. He wanted to tell April she had helped so much, but that had to wait until they were alone. With Belle present, it might seem to her as if his response had been spoon-fed to him by April.

Still, he wished he could say something to let her know what a big help she had been. Or just lock her in his arms for a hug too?

He cleared his throat uncomfortably. "Can I do something? Oh, the table is set already. Good thing Dad is eating out with his bingo buddies or he would complain about this spicy food. He doesn't eat anything he doesn't know." He was sort of rambling, but anything to get back to normal.

April put the pan with stew on the table and Belle passed around the wraps from the oven. They sat down to eat without mentioning last night again, or the painful message about the bet. Matt knew he could talk about that later. Right now everything was exactly as it should be. And he intended to enjoy that feeling, let it seep into his very core. Store it so he could go back to it later, reach into it again in another situation when things were hard and his little girl seemed so far away he could never find her again. He now knew he could do it and he would forever cherish these moments.

He owed April for having led him to this. Without lengthy explanations. With a...

soft touch? Yes, that was how it felt. As if she had changed his views of the situation, without him even knowing or understanding how she had done that. Maybe because she encouraged him not to analyze everything, but to act more from his instincts? Because she urged him to trust his gut feelings? To value his heart over his head?

It seemed like a risky proposition, but if it worked…

Maybe he needed more of that in his life.

CHAPTER NINE

APRIL SAT AT the kitchen table and spooned ice cream straight from the tub. It was ironic that it was Belle who'd had her heart broken and here she was doing what people were supposed to do after a breakup. But lying on her bed, she had realized she had never eaten a tub of ice cream after Matt had sacked her so right now might be as good a moment for it as ever. Especially as she was eating it in his home.

She was actually back in his home. Years ago she had never thought she would return here, not even for a casual visit. She had longed to stay as far away as she could to prevent the hurting. But now she had bitten the bullet for her own sake, to finally deal with all these emotions and move on, give herself a chance to leave behind the fantasy of Matt and her together and open her heart to the future. A future on her own, devoted to her career, or maybe with a new love. Anything was possible. That kind of freedom opened up a large window of opportunity and that was exciting. She should sit here and make plans, indulge in her freedom.

Instead, she felt kind of…comfortable, right here. She wasn't thinking of places to go and people to meet. No. She liked it right here. And she wanted to sink into this feeling of…belonging?

Uh-oh.

April scooped more triple chocolate ice cream and let it melt on her tongue. This was dangerous. She was getting comfortable with Matt and that was…well, probably even worse than being uncomfortable. Because when she had stayed away from him she had been able to dislike him for what he had done back then, while now she liked him for the way he cared for his daughter and his guests and how hard he worked and…

Her phone beeped. A message from David, a guy she worked with a lot on the ship. He wanted to know if she had a moment to videocall. She agreed and his tanned face filled her screen. "Hey, April." He grinned. "I have no idea what time it is where you are. Probably late. I'm sorry."

"Sure you are." April held up a spoonful of ice cream so he could see it. "Midnight snack."

"Happy New Year." David held up an energy bar. "I'm sitting in the sunshine on a mountain peak in New Zealand. I started climbing as soon as it got light. It was pretty tough." He held his hand closer to the screen and she saw blisters on his palm. "I was wearing new gloves and they're different from the old ones. But everything else is fine."

"Are you by yourself or with friends?"

"By myself. Hiking for a few days. Bliss." David closed his eyes with an exaggerated expression of joy. "On the ship you can never be alone. I mean, I could lock myself in my cabin for an hour but even then... Here there are no sounds but a bird of prey soaring overhead. It's great."

"Glad you're having fun. How did you celebrate the New Year?"

"I sat at my campfire and watched the sparks jump away from the logs and die in the air. It looked a lot like fireworks if you have enough imagination."

April nodded while spooning more ice cream.

David asked, "And how is my favorite one-stripe officer doing? Did you party last night?"

"Yeah, there were big celebrations in town. Food, dancing, fireworks. I had a good time. Being with my family again… My sister had another baby three months ago and I hadn't even seen him yet."

"The toll of cruise ship life. Hey, look at this view…" David held his phone away from his face and filmed the surroundings. April whistled at the stunning view down the valley. "That is amazing."

"Told you, you should come this way some time. It's so worth it." David waited a few moments and then said, "You have a six week leave. You could come over for two weeks."

"I guess." April slowly licked the spoon. The metal was ice cold. Did she want to use her leave to explore the world? Or to be here, in Heartmont? Reconnecting with people who meant the world to her?

David said, "Think about it, okay? I'm going to take a few more photos and then hike back down. I saw a river on the other side that I want to follow for a stretch. Might give me a chance to spot wildlife."

"Have fun. And send me a few photos when you have the time."

"Will do."

The connection was broken and April put down the phone. Suddenly it was so very quiet in the kitchen. She didn't hear a single sound. She might as well have sat in an empty universe, among the ice-blue stars. She dropped the spoon in the tub and wrapped her arms around her shoulders for a moment.

"Can't sleep?" a voice asked softly.

She jerked up and looked over her shoulder at Matt who stood in the doorway. He wore a gray T-shirt and old stone-washed jeans. There was a bit of straw caught in his hair.

"Have you been working in the stables so late?" she asked, surprised.

He shrugged. "Not because I had to, but because it makes me feel better. Whenever life is hard, I try to work through it. Literally."

"I see." April held up her spoon. "My method doesn't cause as much sweat and muscle ache."

"Maybe I should try it…" Matt went to the sink to wash his hands.

"Why don't you? There is plenty left."

Matt dried his hands on the towel. His back was turned to her and April was certain for a moment that he wouldn't take her offer because he had to be very tired and ready for bed. But Matt put the towel away, opened the drawer, pulled out a spoon and came to the table. He sat down opposite her and she shoved the tub toward him. He tilted it and dug in the spoon. Nodding at her phone, he said, "You had company?"

April leaned back and shrugged. "A colleague. David is spending his leave in New Zealand, hiking and mountaineering. I was a bit jealous. The views were stunning."

"The Rockies are not far from here. You can hike all you want there. Great views too."

"Yeah, I guess." She fell silent, hoping he would say he could take her there sometime.

She would love to do some hiking with him. But he stared into the tub as if something amazing was to be seen there.

April suppressed a sigh. *Could be better this way*, she tried to tell herself without much conviction. *Focus on being friends, nothing more.* "Maybe I can take Belle, for a distraction."

Matt gobbled down a few spoonfuls of ice cream and then said, "What are we going to do about that boy? I mean, we are going to do something? We can't just let him get away with it, new phone in his pocket."

His word choice almost made April laugh out loud. But the situation was far from funny and she said, seriously, "I promised Belle I would look into it. Try to find out the truth about the bet and the promised phone. Who set it up and who took the photo… You know."

"You think that is going to help? Like a neat little police investigation?"

"What do you think? Go see the kid and shake him?" She didn't want to suggest anything more physical than that. She knew Matt had the good sense to check his anger.

Matt sighed. "I know it's better if I don't

confront him. I would probably get emotional and say things I'll regret. I looked online for what other folks do when their children face something similar and you know what it said on those forums? It's just something they have to go through—you shouldn't make it too big. Disappointments are part of life and more of those clichés. But I can't help being mad when my little girl gets hurt like that."

April felt sad that Matt didn't have someone to discuss this with, that he had to dive into the internet for advice. Which wasn't usually the best place to find clear answers. Everybody had an opinion and... She reached for the hand that rested on the table. "Look, we can work it out together. First get a clear idea of what happened and then..." She held his gaze. "You do want to know what happened?"

"I'm not sure. I'm afraid that we might learn more about Belle's classmates' opinions of her that will only damage her self-esteem further."

"Not necessarily. You see, it's so important for her to determine who she wants to be and what the foundation for her choices should be. If her classmates call her names because of her choices, she should ask herself how she feels about that—does she want to adjust to their standards or stick to her own beliefs? That is crucial for the rest of her life. To learn not to bend under pressure but follow your own path. Yes, it hurts now, but if she makes choices she doesn't fully agree with, it's going to harm her much more, in the long run."

"Exactly." Matt stared into her eyes. "How do you always know what to say? To find those words I am looking for?"

April felt the warmth of his hand under hers. She wanted these moments to last forever. Just the two of them at the kitchen table having a heart-to-heart. Sharing their feelings, without wondering if it was odd. It felt right. So right.

MATT LET HIS gaze roam April's features. He had forgotten how good it was to talk to her and how wise she was. Even back when she had been much younger she had judged situations with insight and saved him from mistakes. She had known what to say and do; she had been there when he needed her. He had…missed her.

The thought slowly unfolded in his mind. He had missed her and he had been sorry that she had left. That he had made her leave. He should never have fired her. But after the accident with Flame Cade had demanded it to prevent April from getting injured again and…it had seemed better to do what her family wanted. Matt had felt so guilty about what had happened and… so afraid to lose April.

He had been afraid enough of losing her that he had sent her away. How contradictory was that. He couldn't explain it to himself, let alone to her. But maybe he should have tried and things would have been different? She wouldn't have left to travel the world; she wouldn't have worked so hard to get a promotion. She would never have met…handsome guys like this David, who invited her to New Zealand.

April hadn't mentioned the invitation when she had answered his question about the call. But Matt had overheard as he stood at the door. As he watched the man on the screen, who was so animated and so…comfortable with April. Not a boyfriend, yet. But what was to come? What did he want to say to her if she did fly out to meet him?

Matt had this uncomfortable itchy feeling inside that he should prevent April from going there. But that was weird. She was allowed to go wherever she wanted. To…be with whomever she wanted.

It isn't like she belongs with me…

Matt widened his eyes a moment and pulled his hand away as if burned. He grabbed the tub of ice cream and started to shovel scoops into his mouth. He needed to cool down. His emotions were getting the better of him. He had slept very little after the New Year's Eve party, had worked hard; he was tired and strained by the thoughtless prank played on his daughter and… He was just not seeing straight. That was why he was suddenly so protective of April.

She leaned back and ran a finger along the table's edge. "I guess I had better turn in. I promised Belle we're going to fulfill a few wishes."

"Wishes?" he repeated.

"Yes, from the library. Patrons wrote down wishes and hung them on the Christmas tree. One wish has been granted by the city council but Belle thought it was rather sad for all the others that weren't fulfilled. So we gathered the cards and we're going to dive in and help the people we can. We already decided before she got the message about Bobby and the bet, but… I think it's just what she needs to feel better. Do something for others." April rose. "Good night, Matt."

"Good night." He looked after her as she left the kitchen. April was like that. Full of bright ideas, kind and considerate, always on her feet for others. Her job was all about giving people a good time. Providing service. He wondered who took care of her. Who made sure *she* was happy…

He stared into the tub that was almost empty now. With a frown he scraped the last bites off the bottom. Did April really need David to give her a nice vacation, all the way in New Zealand? Or could she have a wonderful time right here? If he made it special for her.

Dinner at that new French restaurant Chez Amis, a trip to the Rockies…

She deserved it. And it would give him

some distraction from the anger over Belle's heartbreak and the exam waiting for him later this month. Yes, distraction would be perfect. Just what he needed.

CHAPTER TEN

"SO FIRST THING we do is collect all the cards with wishes for tangible gifts like flower baskets or a free meal." April gestured across the red cards she had spread out on the kitchen table. "To see if we can fulfill some with little to no budget. I mean, I can put in some of my own money but we don't have a ton to spend. So we have to be clever about it and combine things."

"How do you mean?" Belle tilted her head. She wore an oversized purple hoodie and dark jeans. Her eyes weren't red rimmed anymore, but the tight lines around her mouth betrayed lingering tension.

"Well, we did have this little boy who wanted a dog and there is a…" April looked for the right card. "Elderly lady who wants company. Now if she happens to have a dog, the little boy could go there and play with her dog and keep her company. I'm looking for matches like that."

"Okay. Smart." Belle gathered some cards and started to read. "Here's someone who wants to learn how to email so she can chat with her grandchildren in Texas. And here is someone who needs a beehive. Oh, this is a special one. Mr. Jeeves has lots of old videos that he wants to digitalize but he doesn't have the right equipment for it. He says there is also material on it relating to the history of Heartmont."

"Hmmm. Could be interesting."

They combed through the cards and had soon made a few combinations. April called the elderly lady looking for company and she turned out not to have one but two dogs. She would love to have a little boy over to play with them. April then called the antique store and spoke to the mother of the boy to get her behind the arrangement. With a smile she disconnected. "She will pick Joey up from school and take him to the elderly lady. That is our first official match."

"I looked online…" Belle held up her phone. "And found someone who is getting rid of all his bee keeping equipment.

We can stop by later today to look at it and purchase what we want."

"We don't know anything about bee keeping," April said. "We better ask Mr. Poultridge to go over so he can judge the material for himself."

April was just punching in Mr. Poultridge's telephone number when Belle's phone beeped. She checked the screen and paled. "It's Bobby. I don't want to talk to him."

"But maybe he wants to explain to you what happened?"

"I…can't." Belle shrank into her hoodie and huddled on the chair. "I don't want to hear his lousy excuses."

April nodded and handed her the telephone number. "Why don't *you* call Mr. Poultridge about the beehive?"

Belle nodded with a pinched expression but as soon as she was chatting to the bee enthusiast, she perked up. "Yes, I'd love that. Thank you. Two thirty? Fine." She lowered the phone. "He wants me to come with him to see all the bee keeping equipment and hear about bees and honey. It should be fun."

"That's great." April pulled another card

toward her. "This is also a good one. It's a suggestion for a Heartmont Highlights tour. A route tourists can follow past landmarks from Heartmont's past and present. The museum and church, the oldest apple orchard, the water mill. I guess it would take a little time to pull together the information on the different sites and combine into a web page. We could incorporate some of the material Mr. Jeeves collected over the years."

Belle nodded. "We could also do an audio tour people can listen to on their phone. You have the perfect voice to narrate the stories."

"Um…" April wasn't too sure but Belle had already moved on. "I know someone whose nephew's parents have a studio. I could ask her if you can do the recording there."

"I have no idea how all of that works."

"But it would be a very nice wish to fulfill. We could donate the audio tour to the entire town. The Christmas tree was put up at the library to give people something fun to engage in after the difficult season with the derecho hitting town last July. The tour can celebrate Heartmont. And also pull in more tourists. It's bigger and better than all those individual wishes. I mean, we can still do those as well, but an audio tour would be an awesome asset to promote the town."

April gave in. "Okay. If you have the connections to get us a studio, I'll do the narrating. But first I need all the information."

"I'm sure you can find some online and there are flyers at the tourist information desk in the town hall. I'll get you all you need." Belle jumped up. "I'll change and get going."

April was happy to see her energized and focusing her attention on doing something constructive. Still, it was bittersweet to go sing the praises of Heartmont while she herself had fled the town and didn't want to live there anymore.

April gathered the cards with a thoughtful expression. She had come here to achieve a clean break with the past. To convince herself that she was no longer attracted to Matt Carpenter. That she wasn't carrying a grudge anymore about how things had turned out.

If she wanted to move on, she had to work through the conflicting emotions that surrounded her childhood here, her time at the hotel ranch, the incident with Flame and her departure. Perhaps it was a good thing that Belle had suggested this project about a town tour. That she could look at what Heartmont had to offer in an objective light. It was a cute little town. It had its attractions. She'd neatly document them, create a tourist trail for the town and then leave to enjoy her own life, her brand new uniform, her hard-earned promotion.

Yes, things were exactly as they should be.

MATT CAME HOME in a hurry having had to do an extra drive into town to exchange the saddle wax he had bought. How on earth had he managed to pick up the wrong jar? He'd been buying this stuff for years. He knew what the jar looked like. And still... Had another customer mixed them up on the shelf? Obviously he wouldn't have...

Or would he? His head was so full with stuff about guests, questions about Belle's mood now that she had suffered such a heartbreaking blow...

And April's presence. Every time she walked through the door, he was amazed she was actually here. That she had agreed to his scheme of staying at his place. And how well she fitted in. It was almost like she hadn't been away at all. As if they could pick up where they had left off and talk about anything.

He felt a closeness with her that he didn't have with anyone else. A special connection. When he was away from the ranch, he looked forward to going home again to see her and ask how her day had been and… It was silly to say he suddenly had someone to come home to, because he had always had Belle and his father, but this was different somehow. So different that he apparently walked about with his head in the clouds and got the wrong saddle wax.

Shaking his head, he got out of the car and saw a young man with dark hair and a friendly face standing on his porch. He had obviously been knocking and now turned around. His face flushing red, he said, "Is Belle home?"

"I guess not. She's busy with a library project." Matt gestured vaguely. "Why don't you give her a call?"

"I tried but she's not answering her phone."

"Oh. How odd. The thing is always glued to her hand and…" Matt froze. He eyed the young man top to bottom. "You're not by any chance Bobby?"

"Yes, sir, I am."

Matt felt anger spark from the core of his being and spread into every inch of him. He stood up straighter. "You have a nerve showing up here."

"But, sir, I wanted to say…"

"Was there a bet going on about kissing my daughter?" Matt asked tightly.

"Yes, sir, but…"

"And did you receive a brand new phone as a reward for kissing her?"

"Yes, sir, but…"

"That's all I need to know. You should be happy that I don't grab you by the collar and throw you out of the yard." Matt tried to speak without his voice shaking. "But I don't want any more trouble. Just go away and never show your face here again. And think about what you did to a poor girl who…" Really cared for you? Nah, he wouldn't give the louse the satisfaction of saying that. "Who is far more than you deserve. Now split."

"But, sir…"

"I said go. Before I lose my temper."

Bobby hung his head and hurried down the porch steps. He grabbed a red mountain bike leaning against the barn door and cycled off at high speed.

Athletic, Matt thought. *Not bad looking either. Called me sir. Guess I could have liked him had he not turned out to be… The gall to admit to my face he got the promised phone!* Muttering to himself about teenagers these days, he entered the barn to put the new saddle wax in place. When he came out again, a blue compact breezed into the yard and April got out. She waved at him. "Hello!" Rounding the car, she came over, her hair waving around her face on the breeze. She always looked radiant as if the sun lived in her features and beamed out of them right into his heart. It melted the anger about Bobby and made him smile.

She gushed, "I rented a car. It's just more convenient for my stay here. There's so much to do."

"To do?" he echoed without understanding.

"Yes, for the wish fulfilling. Belle came up

with the best idea ever. I won't tell you much about it yet. It's a surprise for the community. You will be so proud of your daughter."

"I already am." Matt straightened up, not knowing if he should say this or not. "Bobby was here."

"When?"

"Just now. He said that he had called Belle and she hadn't answered the call."

"I was present when he called. She cringed." April's expression twitched as if she felt the hurt personally. "She doesn't want to talk to him, while I think she should. She should know more."

"I asked him if there was a bet and he confirmed it. I also asked him if a phone was delivered to him as a reward and it was. So it seems clear enough. I told him to get out and not come back."

"Did you ask him who took the photo?"

"Does it matter? He was 'yes, sir, butting' me a lot but…"

April's brows drew together. She closed in on him and asked, "Just how much time did you give him to explain anything, Matt Carpenter?"

The probing look in her eyes made him

squirm a little. "I didn't have to know any more. He treated her shamefully."

April sighed. "Did you give him a chance to say anything but 'yes, sir, but'…?"

"Uh, no. And I don't regret it for a second."

April shook her head. "You're something. I've been meaning to talk to Bobby and I arrive too late to do it while you get that opportunity and botch it."

"I didn't do anything wrong," Matt protested. "The guy I could just throttle shows up in my yard and I told him very politely and without even raising my voice to leave. I think I handled it admirably for a father in my position." She could have said she appreciated his self-control.

"I guess." April gave him a pat on the arm as if he was a poor soul who didn't get the point. "Never mind. I'll go after him. Was he driving?"

"No, he probably doesn't have a license yet. A red mountain bike."

"And what direction did he go in?"

Matt pointed. April returned to her little car and drove off.

Matt shook his head. It beat him what

she wanted with that boy. The situation was crystal clear to him. Bet, reward, humiliation for his daughter. He'd better go inside and cook Belle's favorite meal for tonight. When April came back, she might want to lend a hand. He wanted her around him, fetching a pan, telling a funny story about cruise ship life, sneaking a bite, smiling at him. Then somewhere along the way he'd ask her out to Chez Amis later this week. A little dinner to thank her for all she had done so far to help Belle. And while they were at Chez Amis, he could make plans with her for hiking in the Rockies.

Yes, there was something he wanted more than anything else. His name on her calendar.

CHAPTER ELEVEN

APRIL DROVE DOWN the road looking for a boy on a red mountain bike. Her heart was pounding at the idea she might hold Belle's happiness in her hands. That she could mess up and make everything worse.

Or save the day.

In her work she often had to resolve issues and it felt good to do so. But it was never personal. This was. In a major way. Belle was more than just a girl she had once cared for. She loved her. She wanted her to be happy. She wanted Matt to be happy. Not to have to worry about his only child being so sad. She wanted to bring a smile to his face that wouldn't fade again so soon. She wanted to see joy in his brown eyes, and…appreciation for her. Hear him say: "It's good you came, April. You are just what we needed. Just what…"

"*I* need?"

She spotted Bobby. He wasn't going fast, but pedaling slowly with his head down as if he was dejected. April carefully drove up beside him and gestured at him to pull over. He looked surprised but did what she asked. She parked the car and got out. "Bobby? I'm April Williams. I'm staying as a guest at the Carpenter ranch hotel. I've known Belle all her life."

"And you're mad at me," Bobby said. He eyed her with an honest direct gaze. "You came out here to tell me how much you hate me. But I didn't know. Honestly."

April blinked. "You didn't know about the bet?"

"Yes, I had heard there was some talk of her being an ice queen and someone having to do something about that but it was never like…" Bobby drew in a frustrated breath. "I never agreed to kiss her in exchange for a phone, you know. I don't know who sent the phone. I asked around but no one knows. Or they won't tell. I bet they're all laughing about us."

He said us. Not me. Not her. Us. April leaned back on her heels. "How do you feel about Belle?"

Bobby blinked. "I, uh…" He turned red to his hair roots. "She, uh…is the cutest girl I ever met. She, uh…"

"Why did you kiss her?"

"Because I wanted to. I wanted to tell her for a long time how I feel about her. It seemed like the perfect moment and…"

"Did you know there was someone watching you to take a photo?"

"No!" Bobby shouted. He was even redder now. "I had no idea. Do you really think I want a photo like that to make the rounds? I would rather crawl in a hole."

"I see. So you kissed her because you genuinely like her?"

"Does it even matter now? She hates me— her dad hates me. He told me to leave or he'd throw me out of the yard. I get that. But I wanted to explain and he didn't even listen." Bobby raked a hand through his hair. "I guess it's all over now, huh? I can't talk to her or to her family. So…"

"You're talking to me now."

Bobby looked her over. "Can you talk to her?"

"I hope so." April gave him a probing

stare. "If you honestly care for her, I want to sort this out."

"How?"

"I bet that somewhere in your class or in the school there is a tech savvy kid. Someone who can trace where the photo came from. Who took it—who sent it. Same goes for the phone you received as 'reward.' Then you have a good lead. An idea who is behind this and why."

Bobby considered this. "I guess there is Jessy Simmons. She's always on her computer. They say she can hack into government computers."

"Well, I don't mean doing anything illegal," April was quick to say. "Just a little tracing, you know?"

"I get it." Bobby seemed to cheer up. "I should have thought of that myself. But I just wanted to tell Belle that…" He hung his head again. "She hates me now."

"She won't hate you anymore if we sort this out. Now I'll give you my phone number and you keep me posted about what you find out. Once we have the whole picture we can take action."

Bobby nodded and put her number in his

phone. "I feel a bit better now," he said as he climbed on his bike again. "Talk later."

April looked after him as he sped away, suddenly eager to get somewhere. To Jessy Simmons? She hoped she was doing the right thing here. Matt was not in the mood to tolerate Bobby near him or Belle. He probably wanted her to forget the boy existed. But was the heartbreak necessary? Or could those two get back together if they found out they had both been deceived?

It was risky and her mouth was dry as she stood there. If the outcome of this little investigation hurt Belle all over again, Matt would hold it against her. And she didn't want him to be mad at her. She wanted him to...

Smile at her and reach out for her and...

No, no, no. Her New Year's resolution was to end things with him. Finally.

Now, everyone knew that keeping New Year's resolutions was hard. The temptation to lapse into old behavior was real. But she had to fight it. Had to be strong. Determined to make this work. For herself, her chances to be happy in her career without that pestering little voice in the back of her head asking her if she had made the right decisions and how her life might have been had Matt…

Life wasn't about what ifs but about reality. And she'd learn to face reality here. One step at a time. She had to cut back on the time spent with Matt. Instead of having dinner with him and Belle tonight, she could go to her family. Ma would be delighted to see her and maybe she'd even have a chance to speak with Cade and ease some of the tension between them. If Lily was still there, she also wanted to talk to her and make friends and show Cade she did care for his girlfriend. Then, from tomorrow on, she'd throw herself fully into the wish fulfilling. Anything to keep her thoughts away from Matt and ensure that her resolution to fall out of love with him worked.

"THANK YOU FOR all the information you gave me about the museum." April shook Mrs. Rivers's hand. It was her second full day spent chasing information for the audio tour she was putting together for Heartmont. It took her all over town to talk to helpful people and reminded her of how willing everyone here was to lend a hand. Heartmont truly was a special place. "And for all the other things about town history you told me." She patted the notebook she was carrying. "I feel like you know every little detail."

"I love history. All kinds of history. I've got shelves full of books and these days I look up a lot online. Museums often share clips of their collections. It's dangerous once I start watching such videos. Before I know it, it's two hours later."

April grinned. "I bet. All of this is really helpful for the audio tour. But as it's still a secret mostly…"

"I won't talk about it. And if you need any more, or run into anything, don't hesitate to call or email me. I'm happy to help." Mrs. Rivers waved at her and turned back in to the museum. It was a modest building a bit hidden away from Main Street and April wagered a lot of tourists who breezed through the town missed it. She was eager to give it a prominent place in the audio tour. All those volunteers had put a lovely exhibition together about town history and the development of the entire area. It also showcased locals who had become famous: politicians, explorers, even an Olympic champion.

I never knew Heartmont was home to such talent.

"April?"

Matt's voice sent that familiar shiver down her spine. She hadn't expected to see him in town, let alone find him…sort of waiting for her? All the meetings for the audio tour were a great excuse not to see him during the day, and last night she had again gone to the Williams ranch for dinner. Ma had been so pleased to see her for a second night in a row, and April had washed up after dinner with Lily, who told her more about her life in Denver and how she had helped out last summer with the fundraising for the town. It was easy to see why Cade had fallen in love with her. With her kindness and down to earth character she fit into their family perfectly. April's initial hesitance had melted and she had found herself laughing and chatting as if she had known Lily much longer.

Afterward she had played a board game with the twins and helped Gina pick out baby clothes from a catalogue. It had been so comfy and eased the tension April felt around Matt. It was funny that she had decided to stay with him to avoid her family and now she went to her family to avoid Matt. But he was just too handsome and too kind. It gave her ideas she should forget. Thoughts about being together that were just…forbidden.

As he crossed the distance to her, that eager expression on his face, she couldn't help but be reminded of a date situation. Him waiting to take her out or…

But it wasn't like that. He would probably ask her who was cooking tonight. Yes, that was it. He had done it last night while she had been away, so it could be her turn now. It felt sort of homey to have a cooking schedule between them.

"I, uh…" Matt hesitated a moment. "I wondered if you'd like to have dinner with me."

A date? Nerves wriggled in her stomach. This wasn't a good idea. She had to put distance between them, not… But she could hardly claim she wanted to go to her family, *again*. Matt knew the relations had been a little strained so it would look strange to suddenly spend a lot of time with them. "Belle is probably waiting for us," she said evasively.

"My dad is cooking for Belle tonight. I told him I had lots of things to do and… Well, I thought it was a nice chance to sort of, uh…catch up away from everything else."

April held his gaze. She wasn't quite sure what he meant. They had caught up, right? They had talked about what their plans were for the New Year and they were sharing responsibility in the situation with Belle and… What else could there be to…?

Had he missed her the past two nights? Had he realized that he wanted to spend time with her? Time away from the others, just the two of them.

The mere idea made her stomach flutter. She tried to tell herself that this was not the way to make her resolution work but her heart didn't want to listen. It sang just because he wanted to spend time with her.

Matt said, "There's a nice new restaurant along the way to Stafford. It has a French menu."

"If it's fancy, I'd need to change." April glanced down at her outfit. She had left her long woolen coat open as she stepped from the museum, so Matt could see that her red blouse and black pants were kind of basic.

But he shook his head. "No need for that. It's all very informal. Just a little dinner to thank you for, uh…involving yourself in my messy life."

"While I stay at your place for free. That almost feels like I should be the one thanking you."

"Then we can both thank each other." Matt's eyes sparkled. "What do you say?"

"Okay, I guess. But I don't know if I can switch off from this project just yet. I've heard so many stories today that my head is spinning." She held up the notebook. "They're for our library project. The wish fulfilling."

"Yes, Belle told me you threw yourself into this with zeal. She was worried it wasn't a real vacation so…"

Aha. Belle had engaged her daddy to take April out, to help her unwind after her busy schedule. That was really sweet of her, but also a bit…awkward? Matt might not really want to take her to dinner and…

Well, if he didn't, he should have told his daughter. I'm not going to second guess everything he says.

"Shall we?" Matt gestured to his SUV parked down the street.

April cast a doubtful look at her rental. "Can I simply leave it here? I don't know if there are any parking restrictions? I don't want to get a ticket. Maybe I can follow you?"

Matt shrugged. "If you want to."

April grimaced to herself as she got into her car and started to follow Matt's vehicle. This was the modern way of dating. Each on your own trying to find a place where you could meet, an hour away from over-full agendas to share a quick bite and hopefully find some common ground. It wasn't romantic at all.

Still she could talk down his invitation all she wanted, but her heart was pounding and her palms were clammy. She was going to spend time with Matt.

Not time over dinner because she happened to stay under his roof. Not time discussing problems and solutions. Not time at a party where they were both invited. No, he had invited her alone. This was just for the two of them. This was special.

Really? She caught her eye in the rearview mirror. *I thought we had decided that romance was a no go.*

Matt turned into a side road and April followed. Another turn, left this time, and they were in a gravel parking lot. She parked her compact beside his SUV and got out. The first flakes of snow were falling from a leaden sky. Matt looked up. "The weather forecast didn't say anything about snow."

April stared at his face as he studied the sky. The flakes attached themselves to his skin and his lashes. She suddenly wished there was a layer of snow on the ground already so she could form snowballs and throw them at him. They could have a snow fight here in the parking lot.

But they were supposed to go to dinner, in a fancy French restaurant, so she'd better behave.

As if he could read her thoughts, he looked

at her and smiled, offering his arm. "Come along, my lady."

They walked to the entrance. It was a large double glass door with gold lettering: Chez Amis. A waiter in a dark suit stood behind a high table checking a reservations book for a couple who had stepped in ahead of them. The man wore a tuxedo and his wife was dressed in a long sparkling gown. The place had a decidedly more sophisticated air than she had expected. "Are you sure we don't need reservations?" April asked hesitantly. If they did and he hadn't arranged for any, they could turn back and avoid raised eyebrows at how underdressed they were.

Matt patted her arm. "Don't worry. It's all very informal." He opened the door for her and let her go inside ahead of him. The waiter looked them over with a quick assessing glance, but only said, "Good evening."

Matt said, "We'd like a table for two."

"Certainly, sir. Would you like to put your coats in the wardrobe?"

"Sure, why not?" Matt shrugged out of his coat. The waiter assisted April and put her woolen coat on a hanger which he handed to a woman who gave her a numbered tag. Matt passed the woman his leather jacket.

The waiter went ahead of them on noiseless rubber soles to a table in the far corner. On each table long white candles were lit. Couples were spooning soup from tiny glasses or trying seafood. The women were all in cocktail dresses or gala gowns, their hair freshly coiffed and their makeup impeccable. April felt seriously underdressed, like a backpacker who had stumbled into a castle.

The waiter gestured for her to sit and pushed her chair into place, then removed himself with a quiet, "I'll get the menus for you."

Matt smiled at her. "Nice little place, right?" He didn't seem to feel hesitant at all. His confidence never ceased to surprise her.

With a wink he leaned closer. "Don't look at all those people who are overdressed for the occasion."

April suppressed a laugh. "They are all overdressed? We are not the oddballs, but they are?" That sure was a way to look at it.

"It helps to go through life that way." Again Matt gave her that conspiratorial wink, then he continued more seriously, "When Chez Amis opened here, I had a very good talk with the owner. I wanted to know exactly what guests can expect when they come here. My guests that is. If I'm to recommend this place, I have to make sure in advance that they won't feel uncomfortable or be overcharged for mediocre food. I found out that although people do dress up to come here to dinner it's not a requirement. And he has a real French chef."

April nodded. The waiter returned with the menus and she accepted hers with a warm, "Merci." She opened it and scanned the starters. Her eyes widened a fraction when she saw the prices. This was not a cheap place. The cities she visited during cruises were always tourist hotspots and that showed in the pricing of everything you could buy there: food, drinks, souvenirs, clothes... So she was used to it. But Matt... She had no doubt he was doing well with the hotel and could afford to splash out once in a while but still... She didn't dare look at him to see if he was cringing.

He claimed to have known all about this place to be able to recommend it, so…she should lean back and enjoy the evening.

MATT CAST HIS eye across the menu. To be honest, he didn't know much about French cuisine and the only thing he particularly noted about the different items was the price tag. But April was used to the best food, on the ship and all over the world. He could hardly have taken her to a hamburger joint. No. This was the thing to do. To treat her to a proper fancy meal. An evening out with no worries. She deserved it.

The waiter came to ask if he could pour them a drink and Matt asked for sparkling water. "We'd better not have any alcohol because we have to drive home safely."

She stared into his eyes. It was as if the word *home* clicked with her. Did she ever wish for a home, away from the ship? Did she ever long to…settle? What was going through her head as she looked at him, or better seemed to stare right through him, lost in thought? It struck him that they had talked a lot since she had come back to town, but he knew so little about her true feelings. About the things that mattered most to her in life. He longed to have her open up to him, not because she was helping him out with his daughter, but because she trusted him and knew she could tell him anything, always.

"April?" Matt reached out and touched her hand. "Is sparkling water okay?"

"Yes, fine. Saves me the trouble of agonizing about what wine goes best with the bouillabaisse."

After the waiter had left, Matt said, "That's why I never offer dinner at the hotel. I'd have to learn a lot about wine and table etiquette and I'm just too lazy for it."

"I don't believe that. You love what you do at the hotel. You would look things up online and master it in a jiffy. I bet you don't do dinner because you don't want to spend half the evening running after your guests and ignoring Belle."

Matt nodded. "Pretty much true." She knew him so well. He wanted to say something light to make conversation, but he didn't seem able to think of anything. He felt hesitance in April's features and posture. As if she wasn't fully sold on this meal. Was it because he had done it half-heartedly, taking her to an expensive res-taurant but not dressing up for the occasion? Did she feel uncomfortable because of the situation? Or would she rather have done something else tonight? Like videochat with this guy, this colleague who was in New Zealand. Who had invited her to join him.

Matt fingered the satin napkin beside his plate. He had decided on this as the first step in his plan to show April the delights of Heartmont, to prove to her she didn't have to travel across the globe to find stun-ning views. Somewhere tonight he had to introduce the idea of a day trip with her to the Rockies. There she could see spectacu-lar mountain sights and frolic in the snow.

But what if she just didn't feel good here anymore? What if she'd rather be some-where else?

"How do you feel about being back here?" he asked carefully. "Was it hard to visit the family ranch?"

April focused on him with a little shock as if she was caught red-handed.

"I mean," he looked for words, "you were

obviously reluctant to go there and…maybe you found that having dinner with them was, uh…challenging?"

"It's better now," she rushed to say. "Ma really wanted me to come and I guess it was a bit silly of me to avoid it. Lily is really nice and little Barry is so sweet." There was a stillness in her face as she paused and considered. Then she said quietly, "I just find it difficult to see the old place. It reminds me of when Dad was still alive and… It's odd since I live on a ship that travels the world and I see a different set of surroundings every few days, but I really don't deal too well with changes."

"You mean big changes." Matt felt a little tightness in his throat. "Irrevocable changes. Like death."

"Yeah." April met his gaze. "There was still so much I had wanted to say to Dad. When I'm home, I wonder…whether it was my fault for never saying it." She blinked.

Matt reached out and touched her hand. "Hey, I didn't mean to make you sad."

"It's okay." April bit her lip. "It's been so long that maybe I should be over it or something…"

Matt shook his head. "Grief never fully goes away. And it doesn't have to. It changed you and that will always be a part of your life. But that's not a bad thing." He squeezed her hand. "You're a very strong woman, April. But you don't always have to be strong. It's okay to…just feel things."

APRIL STARED INTO Matt's deep brown eyes. Was it okay to feel things? Was it okay to let down her guard? Or was it just dangerous and risky and foolish? Because making herself vulnerable could mean she'd get hurt. Again.

The last time had been bad. Matt's decision not to accept her apologies over the Flame incident and fire her anyway was heartbreaking. She had made a mistake, yes, but did he have to punish her for it in that manner? He had later explained he had also felt bad about his part in it, but she was never fully convinced. The way she had left kept bothering her. There was something he hadn't said to her, something that had motivated him to distance himself from her.

Now opening up might lead to even worse

heartbreak. She was older; she should be wiser. She should have been over Matt already and…

Why was she doing this to herself?

Why was *he* doing it to her, being so nice and considerate?

The waiter interrupted with the drinks and April was glad she could pick up her glass and sip. The cool glass under her fingertips returned some common sense to her flustered brain. Matt was just being friendly to her. He felt he owed her this dinner because she was helping him out with Belle. It was a gesture between friends. She had to stop thinking it meant anything.

Matt might call her a strong woman, but he didn't really see her as a woman. She bet that deep inside him she was still that quiet twenty-one-year-old girl to him, the loyal helper at his reception desk, the town tomboy? Little April.

Suddenly she wished she had glammed up for the night. A dress, heels, makeup. The works. But Matt hadn't thought it was necessary. He felt comfortable with her like you feel comfortable in a well worn pair of shoes. Not a flattering comparison but accurate.

And she wasn't ready to lose a friend, a dear friend at that, by pushing for something that was simply out of reach. He wanted her to have this night, eating together, enjoying each other's company. She should take it for what it was. No questions asked.

CHAPTER TWELVE

"AND THIS IS the little kid I mentioned earlier." Matt held out his phone to her so she could look at a short video of a little boy playing football. He had this serious expression on his face that made her smile. "He's talented," she commented.

"He really is. I've been giving him some extra attention to improve his game. Also…" Matt's smile faded a little as his gaze turned pensive.

"Also?" April repeated encouragingly. She still held his phone but her full attention was on his face, on the conflicting emotions she saw there. As if he was considering whether he could share with her?

The idea that he was struggling with something but not telling her hurt. Why would he be reluctant? She had always proved to be a solid friend to him. And he had told her about Belle's troubles without hesitance.

Matt made a hand gesture as if he wanted to wave something away. "It's nothing special. His father died about ten months ago and it's been a rough time for him. Football is a nice distraction."

"I can imagine." She took a moment to savor the last bite of crème brûlée. The main course of steak au poivre had been delicious, but this dessert was truly a work of art. Matt was staring down at his empty plate. She probed gently, "Do you feel like you should do more for him than you're able to?"

Matt looked up, his eyes narrowing. "Why would you think so?"

"Because you obviously feel very involved in his case. I mean, you're taking his situation to heart and…"

Matt took a deep breath. "Last week out of the blue he asked me whether I couldn't become his father."

April blinked. "To do that you'd have to get together with his mother. Do you even know her?" For a moment she feared that while giving those extra lessons to the boy Matt had grown close to the mother and that had prompted the child's suggestion.

How would she feel if he confessed to her he was in love with someone else? Maybe he'd even ask for tips on how to handle it. The mere idea made her stomach churn.

"I talk to her when she comes to pick the boy up after practice but... Nothing special there."

Oh. Okay. Calm down. "Maybe you're just not aware of your charm." April tried to make it sound light. "You were friendly to her and her son mistook it for something more."

Matt shook his head. "I don't think he saw anything even remotely romantic between the two of us. He just misses his father and he desperately wants to have a father figure back in his life. I had to disappoint him. That was hard, you know."

April nodded. "How did he respond?"

"He said that his mother was alone and I was alone so we might as well get together." Matt laughed ruefully. "He didn't seem to understand it doesn't work that way. That you can't force feelings."

April's throat was tight for a moment. She was still in love with Matt. Her resolution hadn't worked at all. On the contrary. The more time she spent with him, the more intense the feeling of connection became. There was no denying that she was still in love with him after all those years but he didn't feel anything romantic for her. And you couldn't force feelings. She couldn't make him love her. Not even if it seemed so right for all parties involved. Belle would love it and…

No. It wasn't right for all parties involved. How could she expect Matt to care for her if he didn't see her as a woman? As relationship material? And how could she even contemplate sacrificing her career? Her one stripe she had worked so hard for? She couldn't let one evening out, the special atmosphere, ruin dreams she had built for years. She shouldn't lose her head.

"I'm sorry I shared it," Matt said softly. "It's really a very personal thing and… The boy can't help that he longs for the way things used to be."

"I understand all about that." April held Matt's gaze. "I also long for the way things used to be. Before my father died and…"

Matt reached out and touched her hand.

His fingertips were warm on her skin. "April…"

For a moment she held her breath, waiting for him to say more. To confess he had been in love with her before he had sent her away.

But no, that was silly. If he had been, surely he would have said something. Surely it would have gone down differently?

"Since you've been with us at the hotel you haven't set a foot in the stables. You haven't been to see the horses. Are you afraid to do so? Because it reminds you of Flame and…"

April stiffened. Flame, the accident, was the last thing she wanted to talk about on this special night.

But Matt pressed on, "You can tell me. I can take it. I know I was in the wrong back then. I didn't explain properly why I didn't want you near Flame and…"

"It doesn't matter anymore," April rushed to say.

Matt squeezed her hand gently. "Really?"

April sucked in air. "It…" His brown eyes questioned her, seemed to search deep inside her. Could she repeat it didn't matter? Repeat words that weren't the full truth?

"I do think about it from time to time," she confessed.

Matt's expression immediately became concerned. "I hope you didn't suffer any lasting injury? I should have asked before, maybe, but I was afraid of what I might hear." He waited a moment and added, "I know it was my fault."

"Your fault? How come? I took Flame for a ride when you had told me, explicitly, not to. It was so clear, and still… I thought I knew better. I wanted to prove to you he wasn't skittish, only reluctant to trust. I was worried you didn't trust him and would in time send him away. Where would he end up then? Maybe he'd never have a good home. I felt sorry for him and… I had the best intentions but…"

She took a deep breath. "I was wrong. I endangered my own safety and his. It could have ended a lot worse than it did."

"To me it was already bad enough. When I found you…" Matt let go of her hand and leaned back against the chair. His eyes were dark. "I blamed myself back then and I still do. It was my horse, my responsibility."

"I went against your orders. I deserved to be sent away." April bit her lip. "Still… I wished you had given me a second chance."

Matt stared at her. "A second chance?" he repeated as if he didn't comprehend the meaning of the words.

"Yes. That you had forgiven me and…" *Taken me back.* April felt a burn behind her eyes. She swallowed hard to stay in control of the situation. She so didn't want to cry. Not now, not here. Not during this all important conversation.

"But I did forgive you. I never…" Matt leaned forward and caught her hand in his again. "I never blamed you for anything, April. Honestly. I thought it was all my fault and Cade also said…"

"Cade is not my nanny. It really irked me at the time how you simply agreed with his opinion that if I stayed on, I'd be hurt again. I had learned my lesson. There wouldn't have been another accident. Why did you listen to Cade's gloomy predictions?"

"Because I was swimming in guilt. I felt so bad about what had happened. I was certain that letting you go was the best thing to do. I thought you also blamed me."

"No, I didn't." Confusion raged through her. How could he have thought that? They had discussed it. "I said *I* was to blame and that I was sorry. Don't you remember?"

"Of course, but…" Matt rubbed his forehead with his free hand. "I was so worked up during that whole conversation that it became a bit of a blur. I didn't listen properly to what you said and I…didn't say what I had to."

April frowned. Her heart hammered and she wasn't sure what to think. "What had you wanted to say to me?"

Matt took a deep breath. "That I was so, so sorry for what happened. That I wanted you to forgive me and…come back."

It seemed as if time stretched between them. April just stared at him, the sincerity in his eyes. He had wanted to say that? He had wanted to ask her to come back? She could have stayed?

She could have…dated him? Explored the attraction she felt to him, maybe even…

Married him?

No, that was silly. He had only meant to

apologize for his mistake with Flame and ask her to keep on working at the hotel. It had been about restoring a professional relationship, not starting anything personal.

Matt said, "I never wanted you to leave. And it was so quiet and lonely after you did."

His grasp around her hand was warm. The feeling trickled into the core of her, dissolving the last ounce of any determination to keep him at a distance. Her resolution to fall out of love with him could go in the bin.

MATT WANTED TO say that he had often considered emailing her. Calling her. Talking it over. Telling her he wanted her to come back to the hotel. But what good would it do to discuss that now? She had left, built a beautiful career in cruising; she was back here temporarily… Was she really interested in an apology for something that happened years ago? Perhaps she wondered why on earth it still mattered to him.

"I just wanted to clear the air," he said hurriedly. "Explain to you how it all played out the way it did. I, uh… I guess I've been hiding behind your brother's interference for too long. I would have disregarded what he wanted, demanded, if I had believed that it was the best thing for you to stay. But I had doubts there."

"You doubted whether I should stay?" April's frown became deeper. "I don't follow."

Matt realized he was getting dangerously close to a confession he should never make. He himself didn't even understand it. What he had felt as he had leaned down beside April, thinking she was seriously wounded or even… Those moments had told him, loud and clear, that April had started to mean a lot more to him than just a staff member at his hotel or a great help with his daughter. That he was…developing feelings for her. And it had scared the wits out of him. He had let her go so he didn't have to face those feelings. And now it was too late to change anything. She had moved on, had gotten promoted. She had a life away from Heartmont, away from him.

"Just look at you now," he said with a forced smile. "Look at what you've become far away from Heartmont. It was a good thing you left and discovered all your talents out there."

It hurt as he said it, and he didn't really mean it. But he couldn't dive into the complicated feelings he had harbored back then. She was leaving again soon and saying anything about what he felt, even hinting at it, would be disastrous. He needed her friendship to straighten things out for Belle, to make his daughter happy again. He shouldn't let something he couldn't even understand ruin that.

"I just want you to know how sorry I was for what happened with Flame. That I take full responsibility for it. I never blamed you. You can go into the barn and look at the horses if you want to. We can even take a ride together sometime. If you feel like it." He smiled at her. "I don't want the past to come between us. It's a long time ago and…"

"I'm glad to hear that. I did feel like I, uh, never quite understood why you sent me away. I thought you did blame me. That you were mad at me." A sad little smile flashed across her features. "It hurt to think you were angry at me."

"But I wasn't. You have to believe me." *I was only angry at myself. Angry for allowing myself to feel again. To feel so much. To risk...* Matt took a deep breath. "Look, we're about done eating. Shall we leave?" He had to get away from the heat in here, the chatter of other diners, the intensity of sitting opposite her and looking straight at her. He wanted out.

"Sure," April said. "I'll just use the restroom before we go." She pushed back her chair.

It was like he got a little more air to breathe. Relieved, he said, "I'll ask for the bill."

As April walked across the room, Matt saw several men following her with their eyes. She wasn't dressed up like the other women, didn't have a sparkling dress on or high heels. But there was a natural grace about her, a sparkle all of her own. He felt strangely protective of her, wanting to shield her from those interested looks. She wasn't up for grabs. She was...

His?

Well, hardly.

He almost shook his head in annoyance

at his own thoughts. This was getting too complicated to do any of them any good.

He gestured for the waiter to hurry with the bill. Yes, he really had to get out of here.

APRIL STOOD IN the ladies room, washing her hands. She cast a look at her reflection in the mirror over the basin. What an odd conversation it had been. On the one hand she was super relieved and happy that Matt didn't blame her for anything, that he never had. Hadn't been mad at her, hadn't sent her away because of her irresponsible behavior. That he had even wanted her to come back.

But at the same time she wasn't sure why he had sent her away at all. He had sort of framed it as if it had been for her own good. To discover her talents and skills, to develop herself away from home. But had Matt really thought about that at the time? "April mustn't stay here, gathering dust at my hotel, I have to send her out into the world…" He couldn't have known she'd go cruising. She hadn't had that dream back then. She had applied for the deckhand job on impulse to get away from Heartmont, from Matt and Cade, whom she also blamed for her dismissal, and from the family ranch where she was constantly reminded how much she missed Dad. She had applied for that job because it had taken her away from everything she wanted to avoid. And only later she had discovered how the work fitted her like a glove. What Matt just said, giving it all the grandeur of conscious choice and amazing opportunities, made no sense. It was so strange. As if, in hindsight, he was trying to find a plausible reason for her leaving.

To cover up what he had really been thinking and feeling?

Now don't you start again, she told her mirror image. *He said he wasn't mad and he never blamed you. You have to believe him. You can safely close the book on that unfortunate incident. All is well now.*

But why then did the nerves jitter in her stomach? Why did she feel like Matt had wanted to flee when he suggested they leave?

That was super weird. He had asked her to come and live at the hotel again. He had asked her out to dinner tonight. That meant he wanted to spend time with her. Not run away from her.

She couldn't shake the impression that he had bucked like a horse seeing danger. Had shied away from her as if it was suddenly dangerous to be near her.

Could it be that…he was also feeling things?

She stared at herself, holding her breath at the idea. Could it be that Matt was falling for her? That now that she was back at his home he suddenly realized what he had missed years earlier?

Or was it merely a physical attraction? Nothing substantial? Nothing he'd act on?

Was it induced by the situation, the touching story he had shared about his football pupils and the little fatherless boy? Was it a fake feeling that would fade in the light of the cold morning?

She shook her head and stood up straight. She had to stop analyzing every little thing. Matt had wanted to clear the air. Well, it was cleared now. No more hard feelings about Flame and the accident. She could simply enjoy her time here. Second guessing his intentions was just creating new tension. And that would be a shame. She had to let it seep in that he had never blamed her. That all her sadness and guilt hadn't been necessary. She should experience the freedom his forgiveness gave her.

She left the restroom. Matt stood waiting for her at the doors leading outside. He stood up straight, his hands in his pockets. He had such nice broad shoulders. He looked so dependable. A man to lean into, to hide with. Someone to rely on. Someone safe.

Matt heard her footfalls and turned to her. The moment their gazes locked, her stomach somersaulted. She felt irrevocably drawn to him. Wanted to run into his arms.

He smiled. "Ready to go? It did snow while we were inside."

She looked through the glass doors. A thick layer of snow coated everything: the ground, the cars. It had even left a white cap on the picket fencing around the parking lot. She made a satisfied sound and rushed outside. She bent down to gather snow in her hands. It was shockingly cold. She formed the snow into a ball and turned to Matt. He gave her a surprised look but she was already throwing. The snow hit him in the chest and burst apart, scattering his coat with white. He said, "Oh no you don't," and leaned down to pick up snow as well.

April quickly formed a new ball. Matt's projectile hit her in the shoulder. The snow breezed across her cheeks. She laughed out loud. She threw a ball at him. He gathered up a handful and came over to her to shower her with it. She ran away laughing. They chased each other through the parking lot, scooping snow off the hoods of cars and off the ground. They were both dusted with snowy patches, water dripping from their hair across their faces.

April halted, panting. Her hands were cold and her lungs burned with the exertion and the intake of the icy air. But this was so much fun. Something she hadn't done in years. Something she only wanted to do with this special man. With Matt.

He closed in on her, holding out a hand full of snow. She didn't run. She stayed in place waiting for him, smiling up at him.

MATT STARED INTO April's beaming face. Her eyes were sparkling. There was snow in her hair, melting into drops that reflected the light of the lamps in the parking lot. She stood as if she didn't want to run anymore. As if she was waiting for him to catch her.

He dropped the snow from his hand to the ground. He reached out to her face, touching her cheek with his fingertips. Trailing them down to her chin. Her eyes widened a fraction. Matt never broke his gaze. He only wanted one thing. To lean down to her and kiss her. To taste her lips and feel how she'd surrender to him. He wanted to scoop her up into his arms and hold her, never letting her go again.

April stepped back, breaking the contact. "We should be getting back to the hotel." Her voice was breathless as if she had run fast. "They won't know where we are."

"I guess you're right." It surprised him how normal he sounded. "Let's get going." He turned away. His heart pounded like a sledgehammer in his chest. He had come so close to doing the forbidden. Crossing a line he had sworn to himself he'd never cross. Him and April, that would simply never work. She had her life away from Heartmont. Besides, she might not even feel what he felt. She had stepped away, had reminded him they had people waiting for them. Perhaps she had realized what he was about to do and didn't want him to. Because they were "just friends"?

He shook his head as he walked to his car and unlocked the door. They had barely cleared up the misunderstanding surrounding Flame and her accident. He shouldn't create new confusion right away. There was nothing between them but friendship. Heartfelt, deep-seated friendship that was worth more than any…attraction. That was what it was. Attraction. Nothing more. He could fight it. He could uproot it. Eradicate it.

APRIL FOLLOWED, hunched in her coat. Now that their snowy fun had ended, she was suddenly cold to her core. She felt so very alone, in the large dark parking lot, as if she was lost. As if she was trying to find her way back after a wrong turn. Her heart ached as if she had been rejected. Still she had been the one to step away when he had wanted…

To kiss her?

No, Matt hadn't wanted anything of the kind. He had brushed his fingers across her cheek as a gentle, tender, kind gesture between friends. Not a lead-up to anything romantic. He wanted to be close to her, share things, as friends did. He didn't want anything else. She had to keep her head together and not mess up the tentative restoration of their bond. She had to carefully keep what she had now and not reach for more...

If she had stood on tiptoe and kissed him, what would have happened? Would he have answered the kiss? Would he have broken away and told her: "Look, April, I think you're a really nice friend but nothing more than that"?

Did she really want to risk it? Go through the pain of such rejection? With any other man it would be humiliating. With Matt it would be outright devastating.

Much more than just the bad feeling of having presumed something more than the other wanted to give you. It would feel like losing a lot that mattered.

The one, even?

April swallowed hard. If Matt was the

one, then the one was now stepping into his car eager to drive off into the night as if he was being chased by a set of vicious hounds. If the prospect of kissing her made him feel that way…

No, she need not make it worse than it was. It was probably just that he had realized his innocent gesture could be mistaken for something else and he had been relieved when she stepped back to avoid an embarrassing scene.

Great that they had each come in their own car. Now she didn't need to get in with him and sit beside him in an awkward silence.

Matt opened the passenger door for her as if he expected her to get in with him anyway. She pointed at her rental. Matt said, "Oh, yeah, I forgot that…" He kept looking at her with a sort of discomfort as he repeated, "I forgot that…"

She rushed to say, "This was so much fun. I haven't frolicked in the snow like that for ages. You?" Before he could even reply, she added, "Sometimes you just need a bit of levity. We talked about such heavy subjects tonight. But that's the way it is between friends. You can open your heart to each other and be very serious, and then go out and have fun together like kids. Right?"

Matt nodded. "Right. See you at the ranch." He got into the SUV and turned the ignition on. April ducked into her car and followed him. Her fingertips tingled from the coldness of the snow.

She had felt compelled to say those words, to sort of establish that whatever they were feeling it was strictly friends stuff. Nothing more. It made the situation less awkward. Important as they lived under the same roof.

But as they moved through the night, his taillights a friendly red glow ahead of her, it felt that by stamping it all as friendship she had betrayed her deepest feelings. Had been totally untrue to her heart.

But what choice did she have? If she opened up to Matt about her feelings for him, she'd lose him.

She had already lost him because he was set on starting his career as a football coach and she was going back to the ship. How could they ever reconcile both their dreams, arrange their busy lives into…?

No. She didn't even want to go there. It

wasn't to be. In the coming days she had to focus on getting the audio tour ready. She had to turn all her collected material into a script and prepare for her recording session. That would keep her busy, so she couldn't fantasize about Matt. She had to enjoy her time out here and then return to her real life. To the future she had built for herself. It had always been like this: she was driving her car, he his. She liked to hold the wheel and make the decisions.

She knew exactly what to expect. No hidden surprises. No heartache.

Just perfect.

CHAPTER THIRTEEN

AND THE LAST bit about the water mill...

April was typing furiously to finish the script she had composed for the audio tour. There had been a lot of work involved in deciding what to include, how to make it attractive to an outside audience, how to present it in the most appealing way and how to ensure that the tour didn't either become long-winded or shortchange the attractions they were seeking to highlight. Her appointment to record the script had been set for after the weekend. She had a knot in her stomach, as she was really not experienced in this, but she'd have to give it her best.

Matt came into the kitchen area and the rush of cold air through the open door reminded her of the moment he had touched her outside the restaurant after their dinner three days ago. Immediately her brain froze, refusing to produce meaningful sentences to add to the text in front of her. Her fingers hovered over the keyboard, cut off from the source of inspiration.

Matt said as he washed his hands at the tap, "Don't let me keep you from working."

Oh no. He had noticed how her typing immediately stopped after his entrance. She flushed. She forced her fingers to type, producing the sound that would reassure him she was continuing to work despite his presence. But there was nothing good coming out. Just repeat sentences that she had written before.

Matt said, "Are you almost done for the day? I wanted to ask you something."

What if he wanted to take her out to dinner again? She was so not ready for another night in his presence. For intimacy that would remind her how much she had missed him and how much she had wanted them to be close as they were now.

It had been a terrible idea to move in here. Should she leave? Go and stay on the ranch with Ma, Cade, Gina and the kids? Ma would certainly welcome it. The two dinners there had gone well but staying full-time would be different from just breezing in for a meal, knowing she could leave again after a few hours. It was easier to manage her feelings that way. She was worried that spending a lot of time on the ranch would reawaken her grief over Dad and her irritation about Cade's decision to go at it alone. Keeping a bit of distance helped to avoid emotional compression that might lead to an outburst she'd later regret.

Matt said, "If it's not a good time to ask…"

"No, it's fine." She cast him a casual glance, then looked closer. There was blood on his left cheek. "What happened to you? You're bleeding."

Matt reached up as if he realized for the first time that there was something wrong with his face. As his fingers touched the graze, he winced. "Oh that. Nothing serious. I wasn't paying attention and I pulled so hard on a bridle strap that was caught that when it suddenly came free it lashed me in the face." He gave her a lopsided grin. "Fortunately, there's nothing wrong with my reflexes so I closed my eyes."

April cringed at the idea of the strap hitting him full in the eye. "You should be careful. And do something about that graze."

"I'll wash it." He gestured defensively as if to ward off any administrations she had in mind.

April remained seated. Everything inside her told her to help him, but if he didn't want her to… After all, Matt had been fiercely independent over the years.

"Isn't Belle with you?" Matt asked. "First she seemed to want to spend a lot of time with you and now she's nowhere in sight anymore." He looked worried as if he thought his daughter was hiding in her room, caught up in her disappointment.

"She's simply busy," April could reassure him. "That's just because of all the wishes we're fulfilling. I'm glad it's so distracting for her. You know…"

"Yes, you were going to find out whether our dear boy Bobby was innocent. But you haven't heard back from him, right?"

April opened her mouth to say it might take more time to track down who had taken the photo and sent the phone as a reward, but Matt didn't give her the time for a reply.

"So I guess he is not innocent after all." He sounded grimly satisfied. "I can't say I'm sorry to hear it. I mean, I would have a hard time trusting someone with my daughter after things began the way they have. The problems a single kiss can create." He rubbed his hands. "Look, I wanted, uh…"

Kiss. Kiss. Kissing Matt. April returned her gaze to her screen, to the mess of words she had added after Matt appeared. She forced herself to read them, even though her mind was a blur. "Yeah?" she asked in a tone of distraction.

SHE'S BUSY—*can't you see? She has so much to do. She kindly stepped in to help your daughter, now the entire town. She has a heart of gold.*

She also wants to help you with that little injury to your face. But you don't want her to.

No. Matt had a feeling it wasn't smart to let her get near him. To feel her soft touch on his cheek and see the concern in her eyes up close. He was just too…conflicted for it. He had to figure out what was going on here. Why April had upset everything in his life. Not just now, but also back then. He just couldn't stop thinking about it. That maybe back then he had already been feeling things for her. That he had denied it all that time. He couldn't hide from the truth anymore. He had to find out what exactly he felt and if she could be feeling something too.

He had to. Even if it scared the wits out of him.

"I, uh…" He cleared his throat. "I wanted to ask you if you'd like to spend Saturday with me, in the Rockies. There's snow there now—we could take a hike and have hot chocolate and you know… Enjoy the surroundings? You've been working too hard."

April hmmm-ed but she kept looking at her screen. He was certain she was going to decline politely. She probably had too much on her plate to spare the time for it. She might not notice that herself, but… It wasn't good for her to sit indoors constantly.

He said hurriedly, "Do me a favor and accept? I feel bad for putting you through so much work on your vacation. I should really do something in return. A little trip so you also have downtime, you know?"

"You don't have to feel obliged."

"I don't feel obliged." *I want to spend time with you away from here. Away from a place where everything is familiar and it feels so oddly comforting to have you around. I want to figure out what you really mean to me.* "I thought it could be fun."

FUN, HUH? April clung to the reality of the words on her screen even though her brain refused to make any sense of them. Matt wanted to take her out to the Rockies. An entire day for the two of them. Away from others, away from distractions. It sounded amazing and at the same time an alarm blared in her head at the idea. She was already falling hard for Matt and now this proposition.

It made no sense either. Why would he first flee the intimacy after their dinner and now suggest...

Because he's just being a good friend. Taking you away from work, providing downtime. He doesn't mean anything romantic. When will you get it through your head?

"Okay I guess," she said. She had no real reason to refuse.

Besides, she had to take this test. Could she spend an entire day with him and not fall deeper? Could she perhaps even dig herself out of the hole she had fallen into? Could she find things about Matt she didn't like? Could she see sides to him that were annoying? Could she even discover that aside from their love of horses and his daughter, they had little in common? After all, it was clear that she loved faraway places and travel and exotic food and Matt was more of a stick with what you know type. And wasn't she cutting him too much slack because of their prior connection? If a guy had taken her on a date and landed them in a fancy restaurant without being dressed for the occasion, wouldn't she have felt terrible and blamed the guy for it?

So anyone else would have looked bad in her book after, anyone except for Matt? Because she had an excuse again? Because she saw all his actions in the light of…love?

"Okay then," Matt said, flexing his hands.

"I look forward to it." And he left the kitchen in a hurry.

Setting this up felt so awkward as if they were a couple of teens trying to go on a first date.

Date?

Suddenly her senses sharpened and she stared at her screen in shock. Could this possibly be a date? Was Matt feeling her out to see if she also had feelings for him? Was he in love with her?

Could it be that he had also asked her to stay here, supposedly to help Belle, but in reality to spend time together?

No. Now she was really tricking herself into believing things that weren't real. Matt had asked her because he needed help with his daughter. It had been a practical request. She need not assume an ulterior motive.

But even then… Matt had initially asked her for Belle's sake, okay, but was it impossible that later, while spending time with her, he had suddenly realized that…

Her heart beat fast. Could it be? Could it be that he was falling for her too? Had he realized it in Chez Amis's parking lot? When he had touched her face, had he suddenly sensed how much he wanted to lean in and…

April buried her face in her hands. This was getting totally out of control. She had wanted to come here to end the thing with Matt, to convince her silly heart that it could never be. That there were no more reasons to cling to the old dream of being with him. In fact, that it was high time to move on.

And now…

Why was he doing this to her? Even if he felt it too, a spark, a click, a connection, how could it ever work out? Their lives were headed in opposite directions. She had so much waiting for her away from Heartmont. She liked to be able to make all the decisions, depend on no one but herself. It was safe.

But lonely. Being with Matt showed her what she might have. She was also bonding again with her family and the town. Fulfilling the wishes connected her in a whole new way with Heartmont and its inhabitants. It showed her that despite her world travel she had a home port to come back to.

She pulled her hands away and took a

deep breath. She didn't know. She couldn't figure it all out in a single afternoon. But she could finish her work so she'd be ready to have fun on Saturday. Whatever else the day might have in store for her, she'd at least see the Rockies again and she did really look forward to that.

CHAPTER FOURTEEN

MATT GENTLY LET the brush wander down
the horse that stood patiently in front of
him. He liked to do this kind of manual
work where he could be one with the animals and let his mind drift. It was the perfect way to unwind after a long day and
empty his head so he could get into bed
and doze off right away. He needed solid
sleep to be able to get up early and serve
the guests.

But tonight his head was just not coop-
erating. Instead of getting into a pleasant
relaxed state where thoughts drifted in and
out, formed and evaporated without him
trying to catch them, it kept offering him
images of April. Like a slide show, with
older shots from years ago when she held
Belle in her lap as she read a book to her
or danced with the little girl in the rain.
More recent memories of April arriving at

the airport, of her cognac sweater at the New Year's Eve party, of the elegant way in which she moved through Chez Amis drawing all eyes her direction.

As one image melted into another, the emotions attached formed into a confusing cocktail. It was tenderness and gratitude for all she had done for his little family after Kennedy had died. It was as if she had become a part of them, a part of him even. But there was also uncertainty, and hesitance, wariness. It was so long ago that he had allowed himself to feel things for a woman. Kennedy had won his heart easily. It had all come naturally, like it had been meant to be. He had chosen her, their marriage, the baby, letting go of the football dreams he had fostered before he had even known her. It had been a sacrifice but one he wanted to make with all of his heart.

Matt ached for the simplicity of the decision, for the straightforwardness in his young mind as he had pushed ahead with a wedding, a vow of forever. He had only been eighteen. *How could you be so young and inexperienced and not ready for so much responsibility and still do it? Jump in without second thoughts and just whole-heartedly give it your best?*

Perhaps exactly because you were young and inexperienced and you didn't fully realize the weight of your decisions yet. Now that he was that much older, he marveled at what he had done, yet knowing he'd do it again. If he still was that golden boy who had never had setbacks in his life. He had been raised in a loving family, with parents who were always there for him; he had never had any big problems, he did okay in school and he was good at football. He easily made friends and once he had fallen head over heels in love, it had been serious right away. Everything had always been easy for him, and he had felt a simple faith in life, in the future, that spurred him on.

But then his mother had passed away unexpectedly shortly after his marriage and she had never had the chance to hold the baby in her arms, the baby she had been so looking forward to. It had hurt deeply, but at least he had had his wife to comfort him, his father to support, and life had gone on, being there for each other, united even more by the birth of Belle. Everything had centered on that little life that gave them so much joy. Until, in one split second, everything had changed. Kennedy had died, leaving him alone with their four-year-old daughter and he had cried in the night, screamed at the sky from which her plane had dropped to the earth, destroying the prettiest gift he had ever been given, the most precious feeling he had ever allowed himself to feel. It had seemed so unfair and so cruel and so...utterly pointless.

Matt rested his forehead against the horse's neck and breathed the animal's warmth and scent into his very core. The raw pain of those days had faded. He could still remember how he had felt, but it didn't knock him off his feet anymore. What hurt today as he stood here was the realization of how much that loss had changed him. How on the surface he had stayed the same man he had been: open and kindhearted and always ready to help others, but on the inside he had locked himself away. It was like there were two Matts. One who did know joy and empathy and who had goals and went after them. But there was also a man hiding deep inside who didn't want to open up anymore. Who stayed aloof to avoid heartbreak.

He had found a way to live and it had been a good life. But today he asked himself what he had lost the day the news reached him of Kennedy's death. She had died, but part of him had died with her. At least that was what he had believed. Today he wondered if that part of him was still alive.

And if it was, if he wanted to do anything with it. Or was he just going to continue the way he had so far? It hadn't been all that bad, really. And pretty safe. Riskfree. He liked it that way.

"Dad?" Belle's voice jolted him. "Are you alright?"

He opened his eyes and looked at her. "Just tired, honey. There's so much to do."

"I know. I'm glad you're taking April out on Saturday. She's also working too hard on the wish fulfilling. I almost think I should never have suggested it." Her eyes begged him to reassure her she hadn't made a huge mistake doing that.

"Of course you shouldn't feel that way," he rushed to say. "April loves work. It would be hard for her to sit around here and just do nothing. Trust me. I know her." He put on a confident smile, wanting to erase the tension from her pale face. "Come here." He reached out and wrapped her in a hug. Holding her close, feeling the tickle of her hair on his cheek, he said, "You didn't do anything wrong, Belle. Not with Bobby either. You fell in love and that is a good thing. You should never be ashamed of that."

Belle sighed heavily. "I wish I had just let it be. You know, not agreed to April looking into it. To discover that it was all different from what I assumed. That was just giving me false hope. I mean, April meant well and I wanted to believe her that there was a chance but… Now it just hurts more."

"I'm sorry, sweetheart." Matt locked his arms tighter around her. In moments like these he wished Kennedy was still alive to help him do this. That she could comfort their daughter and talk to her about matters of the heart. He felt at a disadvantage. Especially because he wasn't exactly an expert about love.

"Belle! Oh, there you are." April came

up to them, with a wide smile. "I have some wonderful news for you. I just hope I, uh... am not interrupting anything?"

Belle shook her head and shuffled her feet. Matt sensed how awkward this was for her facing April right now and quickly said, "Just a little father-daughter moment. What is the good news?"

April held up her phone. "I just found out how things happened with the photograph. Someone tech savvy looked into it and the photograph was taken by a girl from your class, Madelyn. She shared it and she also bought the phone that was sent to Bobby. There had never been an actual detailed wager with a phone as promise. She only made it look that way to break you apart. Out of jealousy."

Unbelievable, Matt thought. What these girls did to bully his daughter.

Belle stared at April. She blinked fast as if processing all of this information. "Bobby never kissed me to get a smartphone?" she asked carefully.

"No. He was as shocked by the post online as you were, and the same when the phone arrived on his doorstep. He never meant to hurt you. He really likes you."

Wait a minute. Matt realized he wasn't quite ready yet for this consequence of April's investigation into the truth.

Belle clasped her hands. "You're sure?"

"Very sure—I've seen the proof of it. I guess that girl didn't realize her actions would leave digital traces. She thought you would never question how it had all gone down and her jealous act would remain hidden."

"I can't believe it…"

April's smile deepened. "You can safely believe it. I heard it from Bobby himself. He looked into it, wanted to know exactly who had framed him and made him look bad to you. He never meant to hurt your feelings, Belle. In fact… He's outside now, waiting for you."

Uh, wait a minute. This is not what I imagined when…

Belle made a little jump. Then she looked at her clothes. "I don't know if…"

"You look fine," April assured her. "Now go to him."

Belle hugged April. "Thanks, you're the best." And she ran out of the barn.

Matt felt like the last signal of the football match had sounded too soon and all the great moves he had in mind to get the win came too late. Belle was rushing to meet this guy and now that nothing stood between them anymore…

April looked at Matt. "I guess you have a right to be angry with me. If you feel like I should have asked for your permission to reveal the findings to her. But…this is the truth and she should know it. Should act on it if she feels like it."

Matt lifted a hand to stop her apology. "Is it the truth? Are you sure? I could barely take her being so sad and I really can't stand her being hurt again." He was grasping at straws.

"It's the truth. I can't guarantee Bobby will never hurt her feelings but he certainly didn't kiss her because of some wager. I can guarantee you that."

Matt nodded. His arms felt suddenly empty and he wished his daughter was still here. Instead she was outside. Kissing a boy?

It felt so odd. He didn't want her to grow up so fast and part of him wanted to go out and pull her away and tell her she was too young for this. But April would never let him and he also knew, deep down inside, there was no way to stop this anymore. It had already happened. She was turning into a woman and he was losing his little girl.

He rubbed his forehead. "Look, I still have a lot to do here… If you don't mind…" He turned his back on April and began brushing the horse again.

APRIL STARED AT MATT. She hadn't expected him to jump for joy at the discovery that Bobby had been an innocent victim as well, but this was rather rude. He had asked her to find out what was bothering Belle and she had handled it pretty well.

Almost perfectly, really.

"What if I do mind?" she asked.

Matt said, "Sorry?"

"You said, 'If you don't mind.' But what if I do mind? What if I don't want you to brush me off like that? 'Oh thanks, April, for having done what I wanted…'"

"You hardly did what I wanted." Frustration edged his voice. "I wanted you to find out what was bothering her and give me back my little girl. Now you've driven her into the arms of a boy who can't be trusted."

"*Driven* her into the arms?" April didn't know what she was hearing here. "Belle is in love with him. Has been for a long time. It's her first big crush, probably. She has a right to find out for herself if he's trustworthy or not. You can't lock her up on the ranch and protect her against every sort of…"

"I'm just doing what I think is right." He sounded brusque now, on the verge of anger.

"But…" She wanted to explain her point of view, but he gave her no chance.

"What do you even know about it? You have no children, no responsibility. You breeze in here for a few weeks, upset our lives and then you go again. You leave us behind."

April blinked at the force behind the words. Did he really feel that way? As if she was some outsider who stirred up trouble only to leave again when things got hard?

"I think that is hardly fair." She was trembling but she forced herself to continue. "I came here without any form of obligation to step in and help you or Belle. I did so because I wanted to. Because I believed we were friends. But if you feel different…"

Matt stood with his back to her, breathing heavily. She couldn't see his expression, couldn't work out what he was feeling. Then again, maybe she had never really known what he was feeling. Because he only showed her the parts of him that he wanted her to see.

"I guess…" She had to take another breath before she could continue, "That I could go and live with my Ma and Cade, if that's better for you." She didn't really want to go to the home ranch, because it was complicated, but not as complicated as this thing with Matt.

"No." He turned around quickly. "You're not walking away, April. Not this time. You're staying to see what happens next. Now that you've made it all so hard with your insistence on giving love a try."

She stared into his eyes. He meant Belle

and Bobby of course but for a heart-stopping moment she believed he actually meant more, meant them. That she had made it hard by coming back and reminding him of what had been between them?

But there hadn't been anything. At least nothing put into words, let alone actions.

She felt utterly confused. Undone. As if some protective layer she had kept around her all the time was suddenly stripped away. She rubbed her shoulder a moment. "I'm cold—I'm going inside."

Matt nodded. "I'll finish up here and then I'm coming as well."

He sounded so normal as if nothing special had just been said. Was it all in her mind? A consequence of her own confused feelings?

April shook her head and hurriedly left the barn. In the yard Belle and Bobby stood by the porch. He had locked his arms around her and was kissing her. Carefully. In that cute slightly awkward way that first or second kisses go. It looked so...wonderfully perfect. Despite all the difficulty, they had found their way back to each other.

Teens could. Because they were eager to jump back in and give it another go.

At her age it was all that much harder. Because you didn't want to get hurt and…

April avoided the happy couple and used the back door to get inside. She went into the pantry and looked in the extra large freezer for a tub of ice cream. She badly needed sweet consolation.

"I'll have to start billing for those," Matt said. She was a little overtaken he had followed her so quickly. Had he seen Belle and Bobby? Was he even more annoyed now and would he take it out on her?

"You're eating my most expensive ice cream," he said, "and not by the scoop, but by the tub."

"That's your own fault." She pulled the lid off and took the tub to the counter, dug through a drawer for the right size of spoon. "You cause all the frustration I have to eat off."

"Really? So it isn't Belle or Bobby or the weird complications of falling in love?"

April looked at Matt. "Is it really that weird? Isn't it perfectly normal to want to be loved?"

"You tell me. I have no idea what is happening in your life in that area."

April held his gaze. Was he just asking her, to her face? Are you involved; is there someone you're seeing? She felt a flush creep up. She fully expected Matt to backpedal and say he didn't need to know. Instead he kept staring at her with that unsettling probing look.

"I am married to my career," she said. "I have to be. You can't work on a ship and have commitments on shore. It's a choice I made a long time ago. And now with my promotion it'll be even worse. Long stretches away, a few weeks leave and then gone again. I mean, that's not ideal for any relationship."

"I see. And you never feel sorry that it is that way?"

April took a deep breath. "Sometimes, maybe, but what is a feeling worth? My career is something solid I can rely on. I worked hard for it. I intend to enjoy it. Besides…" She waited a moment. "Why fall in love and make yourself so vulnerable?"

The question was out, hung suspended between them. Matt seemed on full alert standing there looking at her as if he saw her for the very first time. She wasn't sure what he was going to say.

If he even was going to say anything at all.

MATT HAD NO idea how they had gotten to this point. Why April had suddenly said it aloud. Why fall in love? Why make yourself vulnerable? Hadn't he been thinking about that? If he wanted to be in love again. If he could do it again, having been hurt so badly before. "I guess I can't answer that one for you." He heard how hoarse his own voice sounded. And what a vague reply it was. "I can only tell you why I chose to do it. A long time ago. Because it seemed to be the very thing that made life worth living. What does it mean if you have a nice business and money to spend, but no one to share it with?"

April took her tub of ice cream to the table, sat down and started to eat. Then she asked, "Do you still miss Kennedy?"

"Yes, of course. She was the love of my life. I will always miss her." Matt went to the sink to wash his hands. "Her death changed my life forever. It will never be the same."

"Belle told me you dated and there was this one woman you saw over a period of time, but she broke it off?"

"She had the courage to take that step and say it would never work. I told Belle that it was because she didn't want to have a hotel and all, but… I didn't really have feelings for her. I liked her and we had things in common. It seemed convenient and… It was my fault really. She was right to break it off. We would only have made each other unhappy." He turned to her. "Now it's your turn, April. You can't fool me by claiming you never meet nice men on the ship. Or good-looking colleagues? Like David?"

"I get along with David fine. I guess he's handsome enough. We share interests in travel and nature. But you need a lot more for love."

"Like what?"

"Like feelings?" She wriggled her brows at him. "I can't make myself feel something I don't."

"Or don't want to feel?" Matt ambled

through the kitchen rearranging objects. "I freely admit that dating is a disaster for me because I am just not open to sharing my life with someone. I mean, it's all nice and good to have a fun night out and chat superficially about work and stuff but… I realized again just now in the barn. You want to discuss Belle with me and I just don't want to. I feel like as her dad I can make all the decisions and I don't have to explain to anyone else why I do what I do." He stopped and looked at her. "Does that make me a bad person? I mean, should I want to get together with someone also for Belle, so she can have a mother figure in her life again?"

APRIL HELD MATT'S GAZE. Did he really expect her to give him advice about his relationship status? She wanted him to stay single of course. But just so she could indulge a silly fantasy they might get together some day? That would be so selfish. "I guess you have to make the decision for yourself, not for your daughter. Belle is old enough to take care of herself now. She doesn't need you the same way she used to."

"Right, and that's why I'm getting my coaching license and moving on to the next step in my life. Pursuing the football dream I lost a long time ago. It feels like something totally for me. It might seem a bit egocentric but…"

"Why? You have done so much to help everyone along. Your father with the hotel here, even as a teen. I know you. You're always sacrificing for other people. Now it's time to take this season for yourself. It's okay, Matt. You don't have to defend that choice. To anyone."

He smiled sadly. "I feel that I do have to. I don't even understand why. But…" He stared at the floor, searching for words.

April let another scoop of ice cream melt in her mouth. She didn't taste much of the strawberry cheesecake flavor because it was extremely cold. And her thoughts were a mess. Still she knew what she had to say. "Matt…could it be that you feel bad about this coaching thing because you gave up your football dream for Kennedy and now that you're picking it back up it's like you're somehow betraying her?"

MATT ALMOST TOOK a step back. April's words seared deep into his mind. Especially the words *betraying her.* "I'd never do anything to betray Kennedy. I love her." He shook his head violently as if to physically remove the possibility from him. "I don't see how you'd get anything like that in your mind."

"Because you sacrificed your personal dreams and ambitions to be with Kennedy, to marry her and start your family. Now by going back to them, it might seem like you want to catch up on that missed opportunity. And that would be perfectly okay. But the human mind is sometimes illogical and it can make you feel guilty while you really shouldn't…"

"Sorry but your analysis is way off." Matt lifted both hands as if to ward off whatever else she might say. "I guess I sort of assumed you'd understand how I felt because you always used to but…"

"That was years ago, Matt. I can't guess your thoughts. You need to tell me. Or not." Her eyes were sad now. "Maybe I'm assuming too much. That you actually want to share things with me."

"I do. I mean, I did, right, with Belle and all."

"Yes, you talked a lot about Belle, and also when we were out to dinner about the boys you coach and how you can help them. Even about a little boy who needs a father. But what do *you* need?"

Matt felt like a spotlight switched on and flooded him, making him the sudden center of attention. *Now come on, say it, man, spit it out. What do you need?*

His head was a muddle of thoughts; he had no idea.

No, that wasn't quite true. There was one word that sang through his confused thoughts. One simple little word.

What do you need?

You. I need you, April. I need you to understand me. I need you to help me. I need you to...

He blinked. Everything inside him fought letting this reality in, accepting that he would actually allow himself to need anyone, to open up completely and let someone near. He might feel attracted to April but that wasn't love. He didn't want love. Not now at this time in his life when he was getting ready to spread his wings and fly. To figure out who he was, what he could still do. A new start.

"Is that boy still out there with Belle? I'd better go and have a look. If he is, they should come inside and spend some time with us. I don't want it to be a sneaky thing—you know. If he's the real deal, he should become part of the family. As soon as possible."

He left in a hurry.

APRIL STARED AT the empty space where Matt had just stood. She should be happy he was suddenly willing to embrace Belle's crush and make Bobby welcome in this house.

But she had the sneaky feeling he had just thrown himself into another project to avoid the question that exposed his weak spot. What do you need? You, Matt Carpenter, in your heart of hearts. Not what does your hotel need, or your father, your daughter, the people in town? No, you!

But he had skillfully avoided an answer.

Or had he known what he wanted to say? I need you to stop grilling me about feelings. I don't like to talk about those. Get off my case.

Something like that.

What had she expected? A clear answer? An admittance even that he needed her?

He sure didn't after tonight. He didn't like Bobby or the reunion with Belle. Or what she had said to him about his choice for coaching being difficult in the light of his past with Kennedy. Had she really used the words *betraying her*?

It was too honest, too direct. One of her faults.

She had thought she could explain to Matt and help him embrace the future he wanted for himself without him feeling the slightest bit of doubt or guilt because of the past. She wanted him to be happy. But she had handled it in such a way that he had only felt attacked, misunderstood and...

Didn't this prove perfectly that she wasn't relationship material? She just couldn't say the right things, touch the right chord. Maybe there were two groups of people: those who just knew how to handle relationships and those who always made a mess of it. And she was firmly in group two.

She sighed and pushed the tub of ice cream away. She'd better get to bed before Bobby and Belle came in. They deserved to spend time with Matt without her interference. She had to keep reminding herself that she had no place here. That she was only staying for a little while. That she was headed for her own life, far away from Heartmont and this wonderful hotel.

CHAPTER FIFTEEN

MATT PARKED THE car and gestured through the windshield at the mountains surrounding them. "Aren't they gorgeous? And fresh snow too. It fell especially for our outing it seems." It had become Saturday much sooner than he had anticipated. He hadn't been able to sleep much and all the way to the starting point of their hiking route, he had talked. Nervously, nonstop. About the weather, local news, the place they were going. He was as jittery as if this was a super important event. And he didn't really want it to be that big. He was just showing a friend around.

But as he rounded the car and opened the passenger door to let April out, he couldn't help noticing how great she looked in a red windbreaker that pushed color into her cheeks. Her eyes were excited and she seemed as eager as he was to get out and explore.

She pulled a woolen hat over her hair and ears. "Better wrap up against the cold, huh?"

"You missed a little there," he said and tucked a strand of hair under her hat. His hand touched her cheek and he saw her eyes widen a fraction. He didn't really know what had gotten into him but he felt almost reckless. Maybe it had been her reply during their discussion of their love lives, or rather lack of, that she didn't want to fall in love because she didn't trust feelings. What if he could make her feel them? Just to show her she wasn't immune to them? Just to get even with her for the havoc she caused in his life. What if he kissed her and she realized that she had feelings for him too?

And then? the voice of realism asked. *Like you two could suddenly be together. She has a few weeks' leave. She has a career to go back to. And your coaching dreams? Will you suddenly shelve those?*

Again?

I don't know. I just don't know anything

anymore. He turned away and pushed his hands into his pockets, plowing through the fresh snow to where the walk started.

APRIL HURRIED AFTER HIM. Matt was sending these mixed messages that super confused her. One moment he was warm and tender, almost flirting with her, the next he was suddenly walking away. Was she imagining things? Was her romantic fantasy getting the better of her? Or was he fighting as hard as she was to keep his feelings under control? To deny he felt anything at all?

She had lost her determination to make her New Year's resolution work. Why was it even so terrible to be in love with Matt? Why should she fight it? Couldn't she allow herself to have a good time? Of course it also had to do with Bobby and Belle, seeing the cuteness of their young love… It made her a bit jealous. She also wanted to feel so limitlessly happy and confident that life was amazing. If only for a while. She'd be sensible again later. Rational and all that.

"Here, we're going to follow those red

signs." Matt pointed them out to her. "Doesn't seem to be too many people around."

"We got the early start. I guess on a Saturday morning people lie in bed a little longer, have a big breakfast maybe. Or if they're locals, they do grocery shopping first and take their kids to sports, before they are free to have downtime."

"But we're breaking free." Matt winked at her. "I've looked forward to this."

"Me too." April looked around her. "If I have one regret during my travels, it's that I don't often see snowcapped mountains. It's a spectacular sight that never fails to impress me."

"I love the mountains," Matt said. His voice was full of awe. "I took Belle out here most every weekend when she was younger. In the summer we camped out and… I just hope she loves those memories as much as I do." He glanced at her. "Perhaps you were right."

"Right about what?"

"That following my own dreams feels like betrayal. Of my father role. As if I am letting Belle down."

Ah. He avoided applying her analysis to

Kennedy and him, to love. He only considered his relationship with Belle. She had to admit he was a clever manipulator to stay away from personally being touched. "And nothing more?" she asked.

He glanced at her again. "What more can there be?"

"You're not just Belle's father."

"Trust me, when you have a child, there is so little time for anything but parenting. It makes it sound awful like it was a dead weight on my life. It wasn't. But you get so stuck in the role. It is hard to see anything else."

"Well, now that she's growing up, you can sort of step away. Not in a major move, but gradually. Let her go into her own future and then also consider yours. Coaching really is a thing you're good at. So it makes sense to take the step from volunteering to starting a career in it. I was just surprised you want to move away from here. I always felt like you belonged in Heartmont."

"I guess it's about time to see a little of the world. You should applaud that. You never wanted to stay in one place."

I did. I always wanted to stay here. In Heartmont. Have my own horse, ride, be with my own family. Close to the ranch that would also be home to me. That was my life's goal when I was little even until I was twenty-one... You were my dream.

"It's funny..." Matt spoke softly. "When I got to know you well, while you took care of Belle and helped me at the hotel, you never told me that you dreamed of traveling. You never mentioned wanting to sail the seven seas or see Australia. I wondered after you had left if...we had ever really been close." He cleared his throat a moment. "I guess I overrated our relationship, right? I was just an employer to you. Your boss."

"No, I..." Could she really say she had never dreamed of faraway places? That cruising had only been second best? It would sound pathetic and besides he'd want to know more and she shouldn't let on how she had really felt.

"I guess the travel bug caught me during my first job in cruising. Before that I didn't really know much about other places, you know. I had to broaden my horizon a bit to appreciate it all."

SEE, SHE FINDS it dull here. Just a small bit of world while she wants to see it all. He clenched his hands into fists. Had he ever thought anything else? It shouldn't come as a shock. It shouldn't make him feel miserable. It wasn't like he was a die-hard Heartmont promotor. He himself was now considering moving on.

"I guess we all change through the years," April said. "And our dreams change too. They have to." It sounded a bit wistful.

He looked at her. "What dream do you wish you could still fulfill?" he asked softly.

She met his gaze and for a moment he was totally lost in her eyes. In the intense honesty in them. The warmth that seemed to reach out to him.

He said, "If you had written a wish on the card for the Christmas tree at the library, what would it have been?"

She didn't respond right away. He brushed his hand quickly against hers. They were both wearing gloves but still he ached for contact. For that heartfelt connection he had sensed earlier.

"You're the loyal wish fulfiller," he said softly. "And I appreciate that so much. But there must also be things you wish for. Things you want." He waited a moment. "You can tell me. I won't share with anyone else. Promise."

APRIL'S HEART POUNDED. Could she simply tell him: I want you?

No, that would be disastrous. He'd stare at her, first puzzled, then understanding, then perhaps pitying? She'd lose everything she valued. She'd rather have this day out with him and nothing more than gamble it all away on the off chance that…

"Look!" She pointed ahead. "A vantage point. Beat you to it!" And she dashed off. She had to run away from him, from the honesty he wanted, the confidences she didn't want to share. Not while she was so vulnerable and could so easily be hurt.

She ran on and stopped to look over her shoulder at him. "Come on! You can't let me win that easily."

MATT WAS OVERTAKEN by her decision to speed off. It was almost like she was hiding something from him. But what?

He watched her cheerful wave. Go after her? Beat her? He broke into a run.

April darted ahead of him. She was light on her feet despite the snow. Her red coat caught the light. Her hair had escaped from her hat again and danced on the breeze. She scampered up a little incline. She was almost there. Then she gave a scream. She slipped and disappeared from his sight.

Matt stared. His heart stopped a moment and then thundered on. "April!" He heard the panic in his voice echo around him. "April! No! April!"

He raced to the spot where he had seen her fall. Had she dropped over a cliff edge? How could he have brought her here? It was all his fault.

He reached the spot and looked down. The path continued with a steep decline, slippery with frozen snow. April lay a few yards away, covered in snow, her arms and legs sprawled out. He raced to her and knelt down. Memories of her fall off Flame assailed him. Then he had believed she was dead. Now he struggled with the panic that she was somehow seriously hurt. He pulled off his glove and touched her face.

Her eyelids fluttered. She muttered, "Don't run on ice." Her eyes opened fully and she focused on him. She forced a brave smile. "I'm fine."

Trying to move, she groaned. Pain flashed across her features.

"Does it hurt that much?" he asked. "Where are you injured?"

She sucked in air. "I just need a moment to catch my breath. The fall knocked the wind out of me." She moved her arms carefully. "Believe me, only my pride got a dent. I feel super silly."

"No, it's fine. I just thought…" He let out a relieved half-laugh. "I couldn't see exactly what happened so… Take your time."

"I really don't want to take my time because all this snow is seeping through my clothes." April struggled to sit up. Her face contorted again. "I think my, uh…ankle got a little twisted when my leg slipped out from under me."

"Left or right?" he asked.

"Left."

"Let me take a look at it." He removed her boot and slipped off her sock. He let his fingers carefully examine her ankle.

With his first aid knowledge, he could easily determine whether there was anything broken. Fortunately not. "Just seems to have taken a bit of impact when you fell. Even if it's not a heavy sprain, it will be tender."

"Oh no." April groaned. "There goes our day in the Rockies. I can't walk like that, right?"

"I guess not. We haven't gone that far luckily, so I just have to support you back to the car."

She flashed her eyes at him. "I can limp my own way back to the car."

"Don't be stubborn. You'll only aggravate the injury and it will take longer to heal. Let me help you."

"I just feel like the biggest fool alive for ruining our day." Now she sounded like she was close to tears.

Matt said, "That happens when you try to beat me."

As he had hoped, it blew her emotion away. "Like I can't beat you. Like you're Superman." April scoffed. "As soon as that ankle of mine is healed, I will show you something."

"You're on. But right now I have to get you back to the car before you freeze to the path. Come on."

APRIL DIDN'T COMMENT as Matt helped her to her feet. She could breathe normally again and aside from her tender ankle, nothing hurt much. She did feel like the klutz of the year to have managed to injure herself on her...date with him?

Nope, it had just been an outing between friends. Nothing more. It was nice to lean on his arm and let him support her back to the car though. Even in her wet clothes and with the uncomfortable chill of the breeze on her she savored the moments. She'd never admit it but she wanted to be close to him. Rely on him. Feel safe in his arms.

Matt said, "Take your time. Don't overdo it. You know, if there wasn't any snow, I'd carry you. It would be that much more convenient for your ankle."

"Yes, but there is snow and if you take a tumble with me in your arms, well, we're going to have a lot of explaining to do when we get home."

Home. She said home. She meant home.

She was thinking of the ranch hotel as her home. Matt as her husband, Belle her daughter and...

But that wasn't real. She was stealing all of it, from Kennedy who still had Matt's heart. Earlier he had said: "I love her." Not loved her, past tense. No, "love her." He still cared so much. Wasn't that beautiful? Love that outlasted death? A man who never wanted to remarry? It was rare, but it happened.

Maybe she should be glad he was so honest about it. That she knew his feelings to a tee. No false hope, no promises, only to admit later: sorry, but you can't live up to her, you can never be to me what she was.

April understood all too well how it felt to ache for the past, for things that had been and gone. Her father, walking in the orchards, her running to him, him turning at the last instant to smile at her. Falling into step with him, not saying anything. They had never had long intense talks. They had understood each other without words.

Knowing how much she still missed Dad because he had got her, in a way nobody else did, April could readily see how Matt believed he'd never meet anyone who was to him what Kennedy had been. A first love, with so many special feelings attached. Something too big and beautiful to ever have anything compare to it.

April couldn't even resent Kennedy. It was so tragic how she had lost her life, had been cheated out of so many years of happiness with Matt. She had lost everything in that instant when her plane had crashed from the sky. She deserved to be remembered with love and joy.

Unlike Kennedy who had never had a chance to grow older, April had spent the years living beautiful experiences all over the world. She should be grateful for everything she had, instead of pining for the one thing she couldn't have. By letting go of her earlier expectations of love and marriage, she'd create space to fully embrace her current life, her promotion, a career path that could lead her to greater achievements. Maybe one day she'd even be captain of her own ship? It was possible if she focused all her energy in the right direction.

She simply had to accept that Matt would never love her. And that the wish he had asked her about right before she had fallen would never come true.

CHAPTER SIXTEEN

"ARE YOU COMFORTABLE?" Matt asked. He rearranged the plaid blanket he had put over April's legs. He had driven her home as fast as he could and she was now on the sofa in his living room, her ankle on a pillow. "I'll make you some coffee. And how about a cinnamon bun? There are a few left of Belle's baking the other day. Unless she ate all of them of course. I'll have a look. Just a minute."

He hurried to the kitchen.

"Don't fuss!" April called after him. He heard laughter in her voice. He was relieved that she wasn't in a lot of pain, and that she wasn't angry at him. He had suggested going to the Rockies, hiking in the snow. Instead of adding to the vacation cheer, this little trip had put her on the couch with her leg up, interfering with all of her plans. On the way back to the hotel she had worriedly said she hoped she would be able to walk again soon as she had things to do next week. He knew that involved the wish fulfilling she was so busy with. Belle had enthused what a surprise it would be for the entire town, a gift to the community. It was like April to be selfless and use her vacation to create something for others.

He felt guilty he had proposed the trip, as if he should have known that she'd fall. Which was strange because April was a good hiker and he had had no reason to assume she'd take a tumble. It seemed almost as if...

Accidents happened to her when he was around?

No, he didn't want to think that. It was illogical. There had simply been ice under the snow and once her foot had slipped away, the tumble had been inevitable.

Still something nagged at the back of his brain. How afraid he had been when she had fallen. How worried that something bad had happened to her. April meant so much to him.

Maybe too much?

He shook his head in annoyance and opened the fridge to look for the leftover cinnamon buns.

APRIL STARED UP at the ceiling. *Great, just great.* She had so much to do and here she was, lying on the sofa in the middle of the day, unable to put her full weight on her left foot. It wasn't a major thing and she should be glad it hadn't been worse, but it was inconvenient. Most of all, it felt super awkward to have Matt care for her. She was usually the one caring for others, seeing to their needs and wants. She wasn't used to being on the receiving end.

Her phone rang and she answered without even looking who it was. "April."

"Gina here. How are you?"

"Gina, hi." April pushed herself up better as if her sister might see that something was wrong with her. "Sorry I didn't call yesterday, but I've been busy."

"So I heard. Something about doing an audio tour for the town?"

"You're not supposed to know about that. I asked everyone involved to keep it an absolute secret."

"A secret? In Heartmont?"

"I see your point." April blew a lock of hair away from her face.

"It's so nice of you to do that for the town. On your vacation."

"I like a little project. Besides, it would be boring to just sit around. How are you? And the baby?"

"Just fine. I wanted to ask if you'd like to come over for dinner again tonight. The girls unearthed more board games in the attic that they want to play with you, and Ma is making her famous lasagna."

"I'd love to but I can't." There was no way she was going home limping and have everyone fuss about her. Most of all, she didn't want to explain where she had sustained the injury. Once Ma and Gina heard she had been in the Rockies, with Matt, they'd assume it had been a date and there would be no end to the veiled questions and suggestions. "I'm super busy with the audio tour. It will be recorded next week and I have to practice so it goes down without a hitch. But I will drop by once I have more time."

"I know." Gina sighed. "But there you are

again, catering to other people's needs by doing that tour for the town. You're always hiding behind work. Cade is just the same so I know how that goes. Seems to run in the family."

April sighed. "I can't change who I am."

"You don't have to." Gina hesitated. "I just wish you were staying here with us, on the ranch, and we were all together, like it used to be in the past. Ma will never say it, but she misses you a lot."

April swallowed a moment. "Look, I would really love to come to dinner tonight but I can't. To tell you the truth, I, uh… I hurt my ankle and I need to stay put."

"Oh. How did you do that?"

"Don't ask. It was really silly. But it's nothing major, just needs rest to heal quickly."

"Okay." Gina sounded hesitant. "Should I come over and visit?"

April could already see Gina rush in carrying some oversized fruit basket or a giant bunch of flowers. Her big sister meant well but April didn't want a fuss. "No, please go and do something fun with the girls on a beautiful Saturday afternoon. I'm fine. I can read or watch TV or whatever. I will come to dinner again, I promise. As soon as the ankle is a little better, okay?"

"Okay. Talk to you soon."

April lowered the phone. Matt stood a few feet away from her with a coffee mug in his hand and a plate with a cinnamon bun. "I could have driven you over tonight."

"I know. But I don't want them to fuss over me. I'm not a little girl anymore." April reached out for the coffee mug. Blowing into the hot contents, she fought the irritation that rushed through her veins. "That goes for you too. You should go see to the stables or whatever else you'd normally be doing on a Saturday afternoon. You don't have to watch over me."

"Do you think it's my fault?"

"What?" She stared into his honest deep brown eyes.

"That you fell."

"Huh? I ran off and lost my balance and you think it was somehow your fault?"

Matt shrugged. "You were so silent on the drive back and… I thought you were mad because your vacation is now ruined. Me and my trip to the Rockies."

April shook her head. "I was just angry

at myself for overlooking the fact that fresh snow can cover icy patches. It was careless." She smiled at him. "Please don't blame yourself."

Matt nodded. "Okay. Thanks." He answered her smile. "I'll go do what I normally do then." He left the room. It seemed suddenly empty. April listened to the silence for a few moments. *Great, now you chased him away.*

She took a careful sip of coffee, then put the mug on the table beside the couch and reached for the cinnamon bun. Chewing ferociously she tried to think of something to pass the time. She had mentioned reading and watching TV to Gina, but she didn't feel like doing anything. She felt cheated out of her carefree day off and now she just wanted to sulk.

It might be childish, but hey, on the ship she always had to take everything in her stride, smile politely, act nice. She could never give her emotions free rein. Here she was at least on her own time. Could do whatever she wanted.

"Aaaaargh!" she said out loud, picked a pillow off the other end of the couch and threw it across the room. It landed in Matt's chair by the fireplace.

Strangely it didn't make her feel much better. The best way to get rid of this type of frustration was to walk a long stretch and kick things, but that scenario wouldn't work with a sore ankle.

"There we are…" Matt came back carrying a stack of books. He deposited them beside his chair by the fireplace. On top was a notebook. "I'm going to do what I'd normally do. Which is studying for my coaching exams. After all, they are next week Friday. The seventeenth."

"That soon already?" April nodded. "Are you nervous?"

"Of course not. I've got everything under control." Matt sat down and opened his notebook. He began to leaf through it with a serious expression. Then he looked at her and grimaced. "Who am I kidding? Of course I'm nervous. It's been ages since I last studied for an exam. What if I go blank, forget everything?"

"You won't." She smiled reassuringly. "You already know lots of that stuff from practice. You're not a newbie at it. So don't talk down about yourself."

Matt leaned back in his chair. "I guess so much I dream of is tied up with getting this right. I can't help but worry it won't work out."

"Of course it will. You're determined to pass and that's most important. Now, is there anything I can help you with? Maybe ask questions to check if you know everything?"

Matt frowned at her. "Oh no. It's your vacation—you're already cheated out of a nice Saturday off—you're *not* going to help me study."

"But I'm super interested in what it's all about. And what else can I do? I don't want to read some dull novel or watch some mindless TV show. I want to do something useful. And fun."

"Studying is not fun." Matt grimaced. "This whole situation reminded me again of how I never was very good at learning stuff from books. I guess I'm too hands on for it."

"Stop stalling and tell me how I can help." She fixated Matt with a convincing stare and he caved, getting up to hand her a few papers. "Here are some questions I wrote down about subjects I seem to do the worst in. Things that constantly slip my mind. Have a look."

April settled into the sofa's soft pillows and arranged the papers. They vaguely smelled of Matt's aftershave. Suddenly it didn't seem to be so bad that they weren't in the Rockies sightseeing. It was warm in here and cozy; she could help him with something that mattered hugely to him. They were together...

That was the main thing. That they were together.

CHAPTER SEVENTEEN

MATT SUSPECTED THAT on her own April would probably have tried to put weight on her ankle sooner than was advisable, but with him around she didn't get a chance. He ran and fetched for her all that weekend and also arranged to take her to the recording studio on Monday when she was scheduled for her audio tour. She warned him it would take a few hours so he looked around the small town where the studio was and had an excellent steak at the local steak house. Then she pinged him on his phone that she was ready. He was about as nervous as she had to have been about how things had gone down.

"So how did it go?" he asked as he let April lean on his arm while they walked to his car. Her face was hot from the heat in the studio but her eyes sparkled, suggesting she had a good time. She was such a ball of energy from dawn to dusk. It never ceased to amaze him. Even with her sore ankle, she never complained or was in a bad mood.

"I had to get used to it at first. Apparently I breathed audibly." April rolled her eyes. "I had to get the hang of reading my text with gusto, without listeners hearing me draw breath every few lines. But it worked out, I guess." She frowned. "It will be hard to please everybody. I mean, some people will say other highlights should have been incorporated, others will think they should have been the voice to read it all and..."

"If you had asked for volunteers for a project like this, everyone would have had some excuse saying they're too busy. Now you've undertaken it for them, they shouldn't complain. They will be thrilled, I'm sure." He opened the door for her. "Careful as you get in. Is your ankle still very sore?"

"It's just stiff. Sitting in the same position for a long time doesn't help."

He waited until she was in the seat and buckled up. Then he closed the door and rounded the car. If someone had told him earlier that he'd have to play driver for someone else, he would have said that he didn't feel like it, didn't have the time for it. Now that it was April, he was happy to do it. Probably because he still felt a tad guilty about how things had gone down. Not for any other reason. Really.

He let out a deep sigh as he turned the ignition on.

"That sounds like the weight of the world is on your shoulders," April said, giving him a probing look.

"At the mercantile I got a long lecture from Mrs. Jenkins about looking after my daughter. She's seen Belle with Bobby, and now she thinks I'm not keeping a close enough eye on 'those young people' as she puts it. I didn't want to tell her much about my daughter's affairs, so I mainly let her talk, but boy, it was exhausting."

"And maybe you also felt she had a point? You yourself said she was too young for a relationship. While these days sixteen really isn't that young anymore."

"I guess so. She will just forever be my little girl."

"And as long as she knows that and she

knows she can confide in you when she has to, it will be fine. Bobby is really nice. Isn't it great to see young love blossom?"

"Hmmm." Matt focused on the road ahead. "What do you say—shall we take home some takeout? Belle is eating at Bobby's place and my dad has dinner with his bingo buddies before they hit the community center. He promised me he'd stay at the hotel reception desk until I was back, but the second I come in, he's off."

"I see. You shouldn't have taken so much time to wait on me today."

"There has to be someone on the premises, in case a guest wants something, but I'm on call." He patted his inner pocket where his phone sat. "It's not a problem really."

APRIL KNOTTED HER FINGERS. Her ankle wasn't all that bad anymore. She could put weight on it without feeling any pain. She had even hazarded a few steps on her own in her bedroom. But she definitely didn't want to overdo it and cause it to get worse. So Matt was her driver and...

Who was she kidding here? She liked

him being her driver. She liked the closeness that came from asking if he could support her as she moved around. She would normally not ask for help. She hated that. But now there was an obvious need so it was natural. And not all that unpleasant.

Which unnerved her. Why would she suddenly become so dependent? On someone who was just a friend, nothing more. Matt had made that clear enough. In fact, the intimacy that grew between them underlined that. No matter how much time they spent together and how close they were, it never came to any…

She turned her head abruptly to look out of the window. She didn't want to think about hugging, kissing or anything like it. That was just make-believe. Matt didn't see her that way.

He stopped the car and got out to get the takeout from a small Asian restaurant. At the last instant he popped his head back in and said he'd surprise her. She nodded agreement.

Alone in the car with his scent swirling around her she pulled out her phone and checked her emails, answered a few questions about the audio tour project. Focusing on practical matters helped to calm the turmoil inside her. She had to stop hiding behind her almost healed ankle and turn back into the strong independent woman she had been when she first came here.

"There we are." Matt hopped back in and put two plastic bags in her lap. They were full of takeout boxes and sent out a delicious spicy smell.

Matt hummed as he turned the ignition back on. The cold air that had rushed in with him warmed up as they drove through the night. April leaned back and sank into the feeling that everything was alright with the world. Tomorrow she'd grow up. Tomorrow she'd face the fact that Matt didn't care for her at all. Not in a romantic sense. Tomorrow she'd tell him her ankle was much better now and she could do things on her own again.

Tomorrow.

Not tonight.

"WHICH ONE OF us gets the very last bite of *babi pangang*?" Matt asked as he held up the almost empty box.

"Not me. I'm so full I couldn't even eat dessert."

"No ice cream?" Matt gave her an exaggerated look of surprise. "Okay then." He pushed the last food container away and sighed happily. "That was excellent. I'm just going to…" He leaned down from his chair to put another log on the fire. Sparks flew in the air.

"We have fake fireplaces on the ship. People love to stare into dancing flames. But it's not like the real thing."

Matt grinned at her. "Want to sit closer?" He got up and came over to her. "I can throw a few pillows on the floor so you're comfy. Blankets and all. Let's do it." Without waiting for her approval he began to create a cozy sitting arrangement right in front of the fireplace. While he was at it, he asked, "Do you want a drink?"

"Now that you mention it…"

"What can I get you?"

"Bitter lemon would be nice."

"On my way." Matt went into the kitchen and came back quickly with two glasses he placed on the fireplace's stone rim. Then he helped April off the couch and onto the pillows on the floor in front of the hearth. He came to sit beside her and pulled a blanket over her legs tucking it in on both sides. Then he handed her a glass and held his up to toast her. "Hey…" His eyes sparkled even more than usual in the glow of the fire. "Remember it was the New Year's Eve party two weeks ago and we toasted each other? Vowing to make our dreams come true this year?"

April nodded. She had promised herself to fall out of love with Matt. That had gone spectacularly wrong. As she sat here, right next to him, having had the loveliest little dinner together and now staring into the flames of a cozily burning fire, she knew she was right where she wanted to be. She could tell herself all these pretty stories about being married to her career and having wanted the promotion so much but apparently there was something she wanted even more. Being with this man.

Matt touched his glass to hers. "To dreams."

April nodded and quickly took a sip. The cold liquid should cool her brain and get some sense back into her. When he had suggested sitting like this, she should have said she was tired and wanted to go to bed. What good could come out of this? In fact…

Matt put his glass away and stared into the fire. It was quiet around them, just a clock ticking somewhere. April realized it was hardly ever quiet on the ship. And she liked it that way. Still, sitting here, looking at the man she had been in love with for as long as she could remember, she wished that this silence was hers, this place was her home and this man was her best friend and her husband and the one she could always turn to, whatever was on her mind. She wished…

Matt looked at her. His eyes widened a fraction. "What are you thinking about?" he asked softly.

She forced a smile. "How different it is out here than on the ship."

Matt held her gaze. "Do you miss it? Count the days until you can leave again?"

She should say yes now. Lie to him. Assure him, and herself. That her life was great, all she wanted.

She shook her head. "Right now I don't miss anything."

Matt kept looking at her, searching deep inside her.

She said, "Right now I am perfectly happy where I am."

Matt waited a moment. "I always knew..." His voice was hoarse. "That you liked this place. And you care so much for Belle."

"Belle isn't here tonight." April heard herself say it. Her heartbeat sped up. What was she doing? Was she actually flirting with him? Did she want him to find out how she felt?

Matt's lips turned up in a lopsided grin. "Neither is my dad." He leaned closer to her, watching her. As if he wanted to imprint every little thing about her on his memory.

MATT HAD NEVER noticed that April's eyes had these little flecks in them. He had never allowed himself to acknowledge, not consciously anyway, how beautiful her smile was. That slow smile that invited him in. She was a very kind person and by nature friendly with people, but still it seemed this smile was just for him. That it was something that belonged to them.

Them. Yes, he knew as he sat here watching her that there had always been a 'them'. Even back when she had come to work for him. He had never wanted to think about it, had suppressed his feelings with all his might. But tonight there was no question about it. He knew and he was no longer forbidding himself to know. April was just special.

He lifted his hand and carefully brushed his fingers across her cheek. From her temple down to her chin. It seemed to take forever and he held his breath as he waited for her to pull back, maybe, or signal in another way she wasn't ready for this. She didn't want it as much as he did.

But she didn't move. Her eyes were filled with a softness, a tenderness that took his breath away. He rubbed his thumb softly over her chin, holding her gaze, wanting to say a million things but not finding the words. His heart was so full.

There was only one thing he could do.

Slowly he leaned in, closing the distance between them. He counted every heartbeat until he was there. Until his lips touched hers.

APRIL KNEW IT was going to happen. At last. After all those years. His lips touched hers in the softest brush like a butterfly's wings on her arm. It was over in an instant as if she had only dreamed it. She didn't want it to end so soon. She couldn't bear to let him step away again. She leaned in and put her lips to his, softly answering his kiss. She closed her eyes and let herself fall into the feeling. It wasn't scary at all. It was amazing. It was all she had ever wanted. It felt so safe, so right. Like it should have been this way from the start. She had always cared for Matt and now Matt also cared for her.

His arms locked around her, safeguarding her from the world outside. This was a circle of light and warmth and belonging from which she never wanted to leave again. She did belong here, she…

Matt let go of her. He moved away from her. He sat up and stared at her with an expression wavering between surprise and shock. "Sorry," he said, "I shouldn't have done that."

"We both did it and it's okay." She reached out to touch his face. "It's okay, Matt."

"No, it's not." He scrambled to get to his feet, sending a pillow sliding across the floor. "I'm sorry—this was totally not my intention—you must understand…"

"Matt, wait!" April wanted to get up as well without asking too much of her ankle. "Wait a sec—I want to explain…"

But he was already out of the room. She heard the backdoor slam.

She lowered herself back in place. Her heart was beating fast and her palms turned clammy. Had he not wanted the kiss? Had she forced herself on him?

No, he had initiated it. But maybe he had only wanted to see if…he felt more for her? Had he wanted to explore his feelings? Had the kiss told him that he wasn't in love with her? That he wanted to be friends, nothing more, that this crossed a line into forbidden territory and…

April used Matt's chair to get to her feet without risking the ankle. She didn't want to hurt herself again and have to depend on his help. No. Tonight would bring clarity. Tonight she would know exactly how it was between them. She wouldn't let him get away.

CHAPTER EIGHTEEN

MATT STOOD IN the stables, leaning his hand against a wooden beam. His head was spinning, and the blood droned in his ears. What had he done? He had broken everything between April and him. They had always been friends, the best of friends, the closest thing he had in this world after Kennedy had died and now...

Yes, he was attracted to her but that hadn't been a reason to go on and... What did he think could happen next? She was only here on leave. She was going again, vanishing from his life. She had dreams far away from Heartmont and...

He wasn't ready to love. It scared the wits out of him. To think he'd let himself fall... No! He shied back from it like a man from the edge of a cliff, knowing that death is waiting for him there. He had to turn back; he had to somehow undo this.

But how?

"Matt."

He didn't turn to look at April. He had thought she wouldn't come out here as she still couldn't walk very well.

"Matt, listen…"

"You don't have to explain," he said quickly. "I'm aware there is a physical attraction between us. And tonight after that nice dinner, the intimate atmosphere got the better of me and I crossed a line I shouldn't have crossed. I can excuse myself saying I'm lonely sometimes, but that won't make it better."

"I'm not angry. I've always known that… there is something between us. Why shouldn't we explore what it is? Where it can take us?"

Because that is dangerous. Because I can't risk being hurt again. Memories crowded him of the moments when he had found April hurt after her fall off of Flame, the scare she had given him slipping away in the Rockies. The pain he had felt then was so real it took his breath away. If he allowed himself to love her and then he lost her again, that would be the end of him. Something he couldn't survive. And he had so much here he needed to protect. The hotel, Dad's life work and Belle, and his coaching ambitions and… Why risk it all for short-term togetherness?

"I just think we should be reasonable, April," he said softly. "We're not teenagers. We're responsible adults. And we know it will never work between us. Because we might be attracted to each other, but…" He forced himself to say it, "There is nothing more."

"Nothing more?" She sounded hurt. "You call our friendship nothing more?"

"That's just it. Our friendship is so precious. I can't risk it by…"

"But sometimes you have to risk things. That kiss felt so right. At least for me. It ended too soon. Why can't we explore our feelings? Give it a chance."

"It's not that easy." He clenched his hands into fists. "I can't…" *Deal with feeling so vulnerable.*

"I do understand, Matt. You still love Kennedy. You told me so. You feel like falling for someone else would be a betrayal of her. You tried with other women before and it failed. But we are different. Our bond is so strong. Isn't it worth a try?" Her voice was pleading. "I really want to."

He turned around and looked at her. "You want to? But how? You're an officer now. Are you just going to give up on that job and sit here in Heartmont, where you never wanted to live?" For a moment hope breathed through him that she'd say, "Yes, I'd sacrifice it all for you." But that was mean and senseless since he had already decided he wasn't going to risk getting together with her.

"I did want to, earlier." She fell silent. "But it's so complicated."

APRIL FOUGHT AGAINST the tears pushing behind her eyes. She didn't want to cry and make Matt feel bad about this. It was her own fault for falling for him even harder than before. She had known it would never work out and still… She had meant it when she had said there had always been something special between them, a connection, and they had to find out what it was, where it could take them.

She could explain to him what she had felt back then and why she had left, but did it even matter anymore? He had said he couldn't love her. Couldn't allow himself to fall in love, to give in to the feeling that he was fighting so hard against because it threatened everything he had worked for. His independence, his coaching dreams. He wanted time in his life for himself and his ambitions. He had earned that too. He had worked so hard for the hotel and to raise his daughter. Now it was his time to shine and chase dreams of his own. If she truly cared for him, she should want what was best for him, not for herself.

"Look, Matt." She tried to sound rational. "I've always felt there was something between us that was…unexplored. No matter how I tried to deny it or step away from it, it kept pulling at me. That was one of the reasons why I agreed to stay here and help you with Belle. You are special to me. Will always be. But you are probably right that this comes at the wrong time in our lives. We are both headed in opposite directions chasing dreams we've fostered for a long time. Besides…our friendship means too much to have it spoiled by one reckless kiss, right?" She knew it was odd that she was suddenly backpedaling after having said out loud she wanted to give whatever it was between them a try. But as he had made it clear he didn't want that, she had to salvage something. It couldn't all go up in flames tonight.

She said softly, "I don't blame you for that kiss, and I was as much a part of it as you were, but as things stand, let's conclude it was a mistake, for so many reasons, and never mention it again. Deal?"

She hoped for one long eager moment he would say: "No, I can't deny this—I can't brush it aside—I can't pretend it never happened." She hoped even though she knew it was pointless because he had already said all there was to say.

"Deal?" she pressed.

Matt nodded. "Deal."

"Good." She turned around and walked away. "Sleep tight."

THAT WAS IT? Sleep tight?

As if he could sleep after this. As if he could rest with the storm raging in his head. With the questions falling over one another.

How was this possible? How could this be happening to them?

He had to acknowledge he had always had feelings for April. Feelings he had wanted to suppress. Because it wasn't the time or the place or… He had been a widower with a young child, not exactly an attractive prospect for a woman her age. She had also worked at his hotel. He was her boss.

And caring had made him vulnerable.

He closed his eyes, stood rigid fighting the pain. He didn't want to feel like this. So exposed, so… April had the ability to come way too close to him, point out things he didn't want to acknowledge to himself. She seemed able to detect what he hid from others; she expected honesty from him about his innermost feelings. And he just couldn't deal with it. He wanted to go on, like he always had, hiding, playing pretend, shying away from what was just too hard to face. A few more days and he'd take the exam, get his coaching license, move on to a new and exciting phase of his life. He had put so much time and energy toward that because he had believed it would give him challenges, freedom and yes, happiness.

He had come so far. Why change tactics now?

He might feel sorry that he had let her go, but it was the best, for both of them. She had also worked hard to get promoted; her career had always been her main focus. She'd also realized that, after the storm of emotions had passed. They had both been vulnerable and given in to the moment, but they were also rational and down to earth enough to realize that life was about more than a mutual attraction.

He held his hands to his face and rubbed his eyes. He was so tired, still so restless he wanted to leave the house and run across the fields. Run until he was too exhausted to think anymore. He had agreed to her deal that they would never mention what had happened again. But how could he face her the next morning knowing he had kissed her and she had kissed him back?

Even with all the rationalizing in the world, how could they go on like nothing had happened? Like it didn't matter and... there weren't any feelings involved? Now that he had kissed her, it seemed like everything he had been trying to suppress had broken free and raged inside him.

He took a deep breath. Why, why had he done this? He had totally messed up everything between them.

Yes, he knew with breathtaking certainty that he had lost her forever. Even if she stayed and worked for the town and baked cookies with Belle and chatted to him, as if it was still two days ago, he'd know it was different. And he'd know he had lost her.

It hurt. But there was no other way.

CHAPTER NINETEEN

APRIL SAT ON the edge of her bed in the bleak light of the following morning. She hadn't slept much and her eyes felt like sandpaper. Her shoulder muscles were sore; her back ached. It was like her entire body strained against the weight of having discovered the night before that Matt didn't want to be with her. She could have seen it coming. And still she had somehow hoped, wished…that love could overcome all obstacles? That it could close the gap between them? Make them less independent or their dreams and ambitions less important? That suddenly with one meeting of their lips everything was different and the path to a future together an easy, open road?

How naive! She hissed in frustration. This was so incredibly wrong. Where was her determination to end her attraction to him? How could her resolution to fall out of love have turned into this mess?

Still, it had one positive outcome. Now she knew a relationship with Matt could never be. That despite the sparks and the attraction Matt wasn't open to it. That he knew, as she knew, that too much separated them. That they were two people who had learned, through hard knocks, to take care of themselves and they were apparently conditioned so thoroughly they couldn't open up to each other in the way needed to make this work. At least they realized that. Hadn't told lies. Hadn't tried only to find out it was hopeless.

No. They had faced up to the situation and said what had to be said. Now she could finally close the book, for good. It was for the best. For all of them. She should also think of Belle and…

She took a deep breath. Part of her knew that she should stay here and act normal and smile at Matt and work through the pain. That would be the best course of action. But the other half of her, the weak and weary half, the half exhausted by the constant fight against her feelings, didn't want to.

After last night, after having been so close, after having tasted his lips, felt his tenderness, she just couldn't have it snatched away from her and then stay around to play the part of a friend. No. It wasn't possible. She had to leave.

For a moment she considered driving across town and turning up at the family ranch. Staying with Ma, Cade, Gina and the girls. They'd welcome her.

But in her emotional state she would just miss Dad all the more, and seeing little Barry would remind her of the dreams she once had of a family, which would forever stay dreams.

April fought her tears. She didn't want to feel this way. She certainly didn't want anyone to notice how she felt. She didn't want to run the risk of crying in front of Ma or Cade and having them ask all the worried questions, press her to tell them what was wrong.

No. She couldn't go to them. She wanted to bring some normality back to her life, some routine she could fall into that would shield her from the turmoil inside. She had to go and do what she was good at, harness willpower to perform.

She had to go back to the ship and… She'd make up some excuse to explain why she had cut short her leave. It was unusual but she had enough credit with her colleagues to pull it off. In fact, she knew, with certainty, they'd be happy to see her and relinquish unpleasant tasks to her. April, the peace maker. April, the problem solver. April, the perfect worker.

She almost felt relieved at the prospect. To feel in charge again, to have everything under control, that was just what she needed.

She started to pack her things. Then she knocked on Belle's bedroom door. The girl answered sleepily. April stepped inside.

"I have something to tell you. I have to leave early. I can't explain all the reasons why—they have to do with work…"

Belle sat up and looked at her. Her expression was hesitant. "Is it because you got promoted? You must have so many new responsibilities now. I don't want you to leave but we can email. A lot, right?"

Belle wrapped her arms around her shoulders. She looked younger in her PJ's with her disheveled hair. The little girl April had once left behind. Now she had to do the same. For the same reason. Flight. Avoidance. Fear of feelings. Of needing anyone.

A little voice whispered to her it was the wrong way. That she was shortchanging Belle. And even herself. That she couldn't run away forever from the reality that she needed people. No matter how much she tried to deny it. She did need people. She wanted to be friends with this teenage girl; she wanted to sit at breakfast with her and Matt.

She clenched her hands into fists, driving her nails into her palms. No. She wasn't going to give in. She had to be strong.

Besides, her decision to leave now was totally different than it had been in the past. Back then she had run in pain over Matt's dismissal. But today she would go by choice, because she had grown up now and seen it would simply never work between them. No matter how much she wanted it to. It was impossible. She wasn't running from anything; she was just facing up to reality. At least her New Year's resolution had brought her that.

"I had hoped," Belle said softly, "that maybe you and Dad…"

April lifted her hand in a flash. "Don't ever say that, Belle. We're just very good friends. Don't make it into any more. Please. That is painful."

"I guess you're right. Still I'm sorry. I wanted you to stay here. We get along so well, and you helped me with Bobby."

"You can email me like you used to. I will always be there for you, Belle." April went to the bed and hugged the girl. It felt so good to hold her a moment and repeat her promise. She meant it, wholeheartedly. "I will always be there for you. You can count on that. Now I must be going."

"This early? Does Dad know?"

"He's probably still in bed. I'll write him a note."

Belle gave her a suspicious look as if she wondered what was going on here.

"Talk to you later," April said and left the room. She carried her suitcase outside and put it in the back of her rental car. She was so glad she had that at her disposal. She'd drop by her family to say a quick goodbye, keep it short so she could hide her sadness from them. Ma wouldn't be happy that she was leaving town so soon but staying was out of the question. Matt might come over to see her and she didn't want to raise any suspicions about what had happened between the two of them. She couldn't stand the idea of whispers or questions from her family. Her heart was raw. She needed to get away and find her feet again. She looked at the house and the stables and silently said goodbye. Her eyes burned, but she was also determined that this was the best thing to do. She didn't need to see Matt again. Everything had been said between them last night.

She got into her car, started the engine and drove off.

MATT DRAGGED HIMSELF from the bathroom, where he had quickly showered and dressed, into the kitchen area. His father was busy making breakfast for the guests. "I won a lawn mower at bingo last night," he said without opening with a *good morning*. "I don't have any use for it, so I traded it for a coffee maker. How do you like it?"

Normally Matt would have said he should

have taken the lawn mower and sold it online as it was worth far more than a coffee maker but this morning he wasn't in
the mood for a discussion and just nodded.
"Great."

His father gave him a thoughtful look
and continued to slice oranges for fresh
juice.

Belle came into the kitchen looking at
her phone. "Can I have a croissant?"

"Just one," Matt said automatically. "They
are there for the guests." He rubbed a hand
over his chin and felt the stubble. He had
forgotten to shave.

Belle leaned against the sink, her thumb
working her phone's keyboard. "Did you
get April's note?"

"What note?" Matt asked.

"The note she was going to leave."

"Oh, has she already gone out to some
town meeting or other?" he asked. A bit of
the tension inside eased. If he didn't have
to see her for a few more hours, he might
be able to cool down and get a grip. Think
of what to say to…smooth things over.

"She left. She said she had something
important to do, for her work."

Matt looked at Belle. "Sorry, what?"

"April packed her things and left this morning. She said it had to do with her job. Did she tell you what it was about exactly? She looked really serious. I wanted to beg her to stay a little longer, but I don't think she could have. I mean, if she could have, she would have, right? No point in me making it even harder on her."

Matt stared at his daughter. His head was empty. He just knew one thing. She had left. She was gone. Just like the other time.

Belle said, "Dad, don't look at me like that. You should know. What did her note say?"

"I haven't seen any note." Matt looked around the kitchen. It wasn't on the sink, or on the fridge or... He snapped at his father, "Did you see it? Put it aside?"

His father raised both arms in a defensive gesture. "I haven't done anything. There was no note I know of."

Matt raced into the living room and checked everywhere. Then he went to his bedroom to see if he had missed a note stuck on the door. Slipped under the door? Nothing.

He came back to the kitchen, his heart hammering in his chest. "Did she say she left a note?"

"Yes."

Matt pulled up his phone. "I'll message her."

"Why not call her?" his father asked. "Then she can tell you where she is."

Matt waved him off and walked outside to have some privacy. His fingers trembled so he could barely type. Hey, April, just heard you left. Where to? What's up? Not about last night, right?

It was a terrible message but he pressed Send anyway. He paced the yard as he waited for her reply. Nothing. She was driving probably, but…

"Mr. Carpenter…" A hotel guest came over and asked about a day trip. Matt forced himself to focus and reply. As he pointed out details on the map the guest showed him, his phone beeped. He almost jumped and wanted to look right away but the guest took precedence. Finally the man was happy with the directions and walked off. Matt scrambled for his phone, almost dropped it and checked the screen.

Just better for all parties involved. Returning to the ship to get back to work early. She's married to work anyway, remember? Take care.

That was it? Married to work. Take care.

Should he feel relieved now that he could avoid a discussion, tears maybe, reproaches? April had simply decided it was better to avoid more complications of their attraction colliding with their common sense. She was always so practical. But that was really no consolation at all. He missed her already. She should be here. He should be able to talk to her. She was worth more than a lousy text exchange and… She had also deserved more of an excuse than he had given her last night. But it was too late for that now. She had left.

Better for everyone. Maybe. April had always been smart. Had taken things in her stride. She was strong, capable, rational, never losing herself in feelings. She would probably not be crying her heart out over him.

He had to look at this from a logical perspective. She had made it easy for him by leaving. No painful encounters, no need to constantly look for a way to defuse tension. No, the problem was neatly solved. April always thought of others, not of herself.

His father came out and asked, "Have you gotten a hold of her?"

"Yes, she had to return to her ship early. Some, uh…emergency."

The lie came out quickly, but his father didn't seem convinced. He eyed him and then said, "So sudden."

"Yeah, emergencies usually happen suddenly." Matt felt irritation that his father was giving him the same disapproving look he had when he had caught Matt sneaking back into the house after curfew. But he was an adult and didn't need to explain himself to his father.

"Let's make sure the guests have breakfast." He turned to go but his father grabbed his arm.

"Matt, you… I thought you had learned your lesson. That you had realized that it was a mistake you let her go before."

Matt held his gaze. He could say a thousand things to that. But he merely said, "Breakfast, Dad," and went inside.

CHAPTER TWENTY

IT WAS TWO O'CLOCK in the morning of the seventeenth and Matt sat hunched over his books, trying to convince himself he knew enough to pass the exam. Yesterday he had been confident that he was well prepared, then while he was getting ready for bed, he had realized he didn't remember a few details from the first aid regulations and had started to rehash all he had to know and…

Frankly his head was now a sieve, not retaining anything. He groaned aloud.

"What will it be?" his father said, coming into the kitchen. "Strong coffee so you can pull an all nighter? Or a quick dive into bed to get some sleep before you have to leave for the exam?" He eyed Matt, clicking his tongue. "I thought you knew better than to leave it all to the last minute."

"I haven't left it to the last minute. I knew it all, by heart, weeks ago. I just…"

"Lost courage?" Dad shook his head. "You should have more faith in yourself, Matt."

"Really?" Matt rubbed his painful eyes. "I haven't done too great lately."

"If you mean with Belle, you were angry about Bobby at first which was understandable. But it's all settled now. They think they are in love and...what can we say?"

Matt was glad his father took his remark to refer to Belle. He shouldn't let his guard down. But he was soooo tired.

"If, however," his father continued, "you mean April... Yes, you did make a mess of that."

Matt sat up straighter. "Dad, I don't want to discuss April. Besides, you have no idea..."

"I don't?" His father stared at him and huffed. "Do you think I simply go about my business ignoring other people? That I am not sensitive to what is unfolding right under my nose? That girl adores you. And you simply let her go."

"She doesn't adore me. And I didn't let her go. She decided of her own accord to leave."

"Oh, you didn't do anything to make her do so? Not one little thing?"

One major thing. That kiss. That wonderful amazing mind-boggling kiss. Matt cleared his throat. "Dad, I'm trying to concentrate here. Or rather, not. I need sleep. I'll turn in now."

"Matt…" His father caught his arm. "I hope you pass the exam. I really do. But running off to become a football coach won't solve your loneliness. You need someone by your side."

Matt looked into his father's concerned eyes. The older man continued, "You have been alone for far too long. I couldn't make you find someone new, but… Then again maybe I didn't have to. When April came… You should see the two of you together. It has always been…"

"Dad, April has a career. She told me she's married to her work. She didn't say anything about us being great together."

"She has feelings for you. Anyone can see that. Maybe she only lied she's married to her work because she was worried you wouldn't be receptive to any, uh, approach on her part."

Not receptive? I kissed her silly.

Matt said, "Look, Dad, this is not the right moment to discuss this. I need all my focus to make the exam. Then I will think about…"

"I only want to see you happy."

"I was very happy with Kennedy. It ended prematurely. After that…"

"You've never been in love again?"

Matt stood. The room suddenly seemed to close in on him. Could he honestly say no? "No, I have never been in love again."

It would be a convenient answer. But it would also be a lie. He had fallen in love again. With April. What was more, he… "I don't want to discuss this. I'm going to bed."

"Alright. Good night." His father sounded resigned. "But I hope you won't delude yourself with this idea you can't love anyone else because it's a lie."

"Good night, Dad," Matt said emphatically and scooped up his books. In his bedroom he dropped onto the bed and stared at the ceiling. He was so full of adrenaline he could never sleep. He'd be wasted and not make the exam and then…

He covered his face with his hands. "It's a lie," his father's voice said. "It's a lie."

No, it wasn't his father's voice. It was his own mind. It was telling him clearly that for all his reasoning that he could never love again, he had fallen for April. He was just too afraid to admit it. To himself, let alone to her.

Because it was too risky. Because he could never stand to lose her. If she came to live here, if she became part of all that he was and then suddenly someday death snatched her like it had Kennedy…

But, a soft voice asked him, *if someone had told you before you wed Kennedy that someday you could lose her and it was better not to marry her at all, would you have agreed? No. You would have said you'd marry her because you loved her. Her and the baby she was carrying. You would have wanted your little family, no matter how long or short it lasted. You would have married her even if it had been for a single day.*

He remembered. With a reality that took his breath away. That was what love felt like. To give everything for the other person. To make them your whole life. To be

there for them, as they were there for you.
It was worth it. It was worth choosing even
for a single day.

One day. But the best day. The ultimate
day.

Goosebumps formed on his arms. If a
phone call came in this moment, asking
him to drop everything and go to April,
because she needed him, he'd do it. He'd
go to her and skip the exam. The exam
that was so important to him that he had
prepped for months. He'd drop it all and go
to her, because she was more important,
because she…

He sat up. The bed creaked under his
weight as if it protested. But Matt now knew
what he had to do. It was so clear to him
as if he had received written instructions.

Priorities. Choices. The truth. He knew
what he had to do and he'd act on it.

CHAPTER TWENTY-ONE

APRIL LOOKED AROUND the large ballroom and pointed out a few minor adjustments to the two stewards who were getting everything ready for the celebrations. A couple on the cruise were celebrating their fortieth wedding anniversary and unbeknownst to them their children and grandchildren had come on board and were going to surprise them with a huge party. It had all been arranged in advance and it was such fun being part of the preparations, while of course making sure the lucky couple didn't suspect a thing.

"The champagne goes over there." She pointed to an oval table. "You can already start building the tower of glasses for it. I'll check with Margery that the city tour is still going. They shouldn't come back early."

She pulled out her phone and checked with her colleague that Mr. and Mrs. Danton were still happily sightseeing. Then she turned to go downstairs to see that the cake was ready and waiting. With four tiers and countless marzipan roses it was a gigantic thing that still had to be moved up to the ballroom. She'd better get a deckhand or two to help with it.

She stopped and stared. The man standing at the top of the stairs. He looked just like Matt. She was staring into the sunshine so perhaps her view was a bit obscured and her eyes conjured up an optical illusion. But as she closed in, the man looked more and more like Matt and by the time she was standing in front of him, she realized that it was…

"What are you doing here?" she asked, her voice breathless with shock. "You can't be here. We're in Acapulco."

"I know." Matt shifted his weight as if he was nervous. There were shadows under his eyes suggesting he had slept badly.

"You should be at the hotel to… No." She had another shock as she realized. Blood rushed to her face. She couldn't believe it. She pulled out her phone again to check the date although she knew it. The seventeenth. "You should be at the exam."

"I know," Matt said. "But I couldn't go."

April blinked. "Couldn't go? How come? Did something happen?" Had he only been allowed on board because there was an emergency? "Is Belle alright? Or is it your father?" Her heart clenched at the idea some disaster had struck while she was away.

"They are fine," he assured her quickly.

"But something pretty serious has to be up if you jumped on a plane last minute to come see me. It must have taken you... what?" She calculated roughly. The drive to Denver, checking in, flight time, then getting to the cruise terminal. "Seven hours? Why would you do that?"

"I came because I wanted to."

"Wanted to?" she echoed, puzzled.

Her phone beeped but she ignored it. "I don't understand, Matt. You should be at the exam. To get your coaching license and start training young people. That is your dream." Before he could reply, she added, "If you just say 'I know,' I will throttle you."

Anger threatened to overtake her ability to speak.

Matt said, "April, calm down and listen for a second."

"No, I won't just listen for a second. How can you throw away a big chance like that? And then pop up here like… Why?"

"Because I want you to know that you matter."

April blinked. "I don't follow."

"I want you to know that you are the most important to me. More important than the hotel. The guests. Or the exam and my coaching dreams. *You* are my top priority." He took a step closer to her. "I should have told you earlier, April. But I was just too confused to make sense of it all. I kept denying that I felt things for you. I kept telling myself we were just friends and I had to be nice to you and… I never wanted to admit how it really was. That I had fallen for you."

April couldn't believe her ears. Matt had fallen for her?

"When you had the accident with Flame, I realized how much you had come to mean to me. How worried I was when I looked for you that you had been hurt bad. I couldn't stand that feeling. I wanted to get away from it. So when Cade urged me to dismiss you, I agreed. I never thought you'd leave town in such a hurry but at the time it was very welcome to me. It solved all the issues in a neat little stroke. I…I was too afraid to admit to myself what I felt or what I truly wanted."

April blinked in disbelief. Back then he had already had feelings for her? Nine years ago?

Matt held her gaze honestly. "I made myself believe that I could live without getting too close to people. I had so many friends and I trained kids and… I had this entire community around me. How could I be lonely? How could I miss anything? Then you came back here and…from the moment we met again, at the airport, I knew that there was something… At first I merely ascribed it to tension, nerves because I was prepping for my exam, getting ready to make a major change in my life. But then I started to see it had to do with you, with an attraction I'd denied. I sensed it but I didn't want to act on it. I was so convinced that I knew what was right for me. For you. For the both of us. I am so sorry that… When we kissed I should have…"

MATT DESPERATELY WANTED to find the right words to say. To give her what she needed from him. He saw in her face how undone she was to find him here, in her world. Had it been a wrong decision? Had he messed up again?

"I don't know how to do this, April." He looked away a moment, unable to go on. "I've forgotten how to do it. When I see my daughter with Bobby, it seems so simple. Reach out and kiss and love each other. But it is hard. When I kissed you, I loved every second of it. But I was also in a panic that I actually allowed myself to fall for you, to feel all these things and… I just couldn't accept it. It still feels surreal."

"Matt." April reached out and touched his arm. "You don't have to explain to me. I know. I'm also afraid. I've loved you for so long."

He blinked. Did she just say she had loved him for so long?

"When I came to work for you, I bonded with your daughter—I formed a little family with you. I grew to consider the hotel my home and… I wanted to stay. But then the accident happened and Cade tried to separate us and you agreed so easily… I knew that you had loved Kennedy too much to ever see me as a potential partner and… I left. I ran. I found a lifestyle that suited me and I was happy, sort of… But there was always you. You and Belle, tugging at my heart. Making me long for a place to call home. When I came on the last day of the year, I made this resolution. That I would finally deal with my infatuation for you. Root it out. Destroy any feeling left. To be able to move on."

Matt took a deep breath. "Did you succeed?"

April's lips curled in a self-deprecatory smile. "Far from it. I fell all over for you. For all the little things I love about you. How you smile, how you talk when you're excited about something, the scent of your aftershave. Everything about you that is just right. I lived under the same roof with you and… How had I ever figured my resolution to fall out of love could work?" She lifted her hands in a gesture of despair. "I couldn't fight it, Matt. I had to get closer to you and… I had to kiss you. And it was everything I wanted. Then you said…" Her expression contorted.

"Forget what I said. I had to push you away—don't you see? I couldn't tell you what I didn't even want to admit to myself. How much you meant to me and…"

"Matt, you said you love Kennedy. Present tense. I don't expect you to ever stop loving her, but… I need to know if there is a place for me in your heart. If you can ever see me as more than a friend or little April…"

"Ever?" he repeated disbelievingly. "How about right now?" And he leaned in and kissed her.

APRIL FELT MATT'S arms lock around her and his lips make contact with hers. She sank into his embrace, feeling the warmth wrap around her and drown out the cold that had lingered inside ever since she had left him. His kiss said everything that his words had been unable to capture: how he loved her, had missed her, wanted to be with her.

She didn't need any more explanations about a past that was done with. She needed him to be here for her, in the now. To convince her that they could be together, against all odds.

He would still have to take his exam, some other day. She'd make sure of that. He was so good with kids, he had to become a coach. But maybe he could become one close to Heartmont. The hotel could be their home base. His father would also like that. And she'd come and see Matt and Belle every few months, as soon as she had leave. They'd make the most of those times, spending as much time together as they could, before being separated again. And somewhere down the road, maybe next year, she'd give up cruising altogether. Because life on shore had its special attractions.

Someone cleared their throat. April broke free from Matt's embrace and saw one of the deckhands she had meant to ask to help with the anniversary cake. He was staring at her. "Sorry," he said. "But we have to get on with the preparations, or we won't be ready when the Dantons return."

"Right." April reached up to check on her hair and straightened her uniform jacket. The deckhand ducked down the stairs to where the cake waited.

Matt touched the one golden stripe on her sleeve. "I'm so very proud of my officer."

April felt like her heart was bursting. "And I'm so very proud to be your girl."

EPILOGUE

"THERE." APRIL TOOK a step back to look at Cade's tie. She had returned to the ranch to celebrate Cade and Lily's wedding. It was only six months since that fateful January leave but her feelings at the time, feelings of confusion and sadness, of tension with her family and Matt, seemed much further in the past. It was all so different now. Her heart was full of peace and joy. And Cade had even asked her for this one-on-one, to help him straighten his tie and get all ready for the big day. Not Ma, not Gina. Her.

The look on her brother's face as he stood there in his wedding day suit almost made her laugh out loud. He looked positively terrified. Big bold Cade who wasn't afraid of anything and always found a solution for everything suddenly seemed... in need of her reassurance? "It's perfectly straight," she said softly, giving him a pat on the chest. "And it's going to be an amazing day."

"I'm so glad you're here, April."

"You're getting married. I wouldn't have stayed away for anything."

"I mean…" He seemed to look for words. The frown over his eyes told her that he was serious about whatever he wanted to say here. Cade wasn't a big talker so when he did decide to open up a little, it had to be about something major. "I made mistakes in the past. I didn't treat you like a grown-up who could make her own decisions. I tried to meddle in your life and… You had every right to be angry at me."

April's heart widened at the realization he would actually acknowledge this. She knew how hard it had to be for him. Her resentment about the past had faded beneath all the happiness she experienced with Matt, and where it might have been impossible six months ago to respond with the same empathy, it now came easily to her. She shook her head. "I'm not angry anymore. I know you meant well."

"You were so young." Cade reached out and caught her hand in his. "I didn't want you to get together with a widower with a young child and… I thought you wanted to help him because you felt sorry for him. I saw all kinds of problems in the future and… I just wanted you to be carefree and happy. I never realized that you really cared for him and he for you. I'm so sorry if I came between you and stood in the way of you getting together earlier. I'm so happy now with Lily, and the idea that I denied you that same happiness…" He swallowed hard.

"Look. Cade, back then…" April frowned hard. She didn't want Cade to be burdened by guilt on his wedding day. This had to be a day of light and happy memories only. "Matt and I weren't ready to admit to each other how we felt. Not even to ourselves, maybe. Your interference didn't break us apart. Our own confusion did."

"Still I want to apologize. On a day like today I realize all the more how important family is. You will always be a part of our family. Whatever happens. You do know that, don't you?"

"I do." April hugged Cade. For a moment she closed her eyes. Cade's confession meant so much to her. That he had thought about it and wanted to reveal his innermost feelings to her. It was hard for him, but he wanted to do it, for her, to be able to get closer to her again.

All was well now. She had come back home to the family she knew loved her. Even if they sometimes showed it in ways she found hard to understand. But she tried to see past what she couldn't make sense of to the love for her beneath.

Cade said, "You'd better go and see if Lily is ready. And keep an eye on the twins. They've been so excited the past few days. They're bound to get into some kind of trouble."

"I'm sure Gina and Ma will also be watching over them." April brushed an imaginary speck of dust off Cade's shoulder. "There, you look perfect." She smiled up at him. "I'm so glad you found someone to love and are getting married now. You and Lily are just perfect for each other."

Cade nodded. He didn't say she and Matt were perfect for each other and April suspected that he still had some trouble getting used to the new situation. But he had reached out to her apologizing for the past and she was more than ready to move on. In time Cade would see that this was the right decision. Besides, he wasn't the only one who was surprised that she was together with Matt. There had been raised eyebrows all over town. But the two of them couldn't care less. They were catching up on all the lost time.

April left Cade and went to the other wing of the ranch house where Ma, Lily's mother and Gina were all fussing over Lily. She looked amazing in a white wedding dress with a wide skirt, embroidered bodice and a lace veil attached to her hair. The bouquet lay ready on the table. The bridesmaids chased each other with a hairbrush and April took a minute to calm them down. Then she told Lily, "Cade is ready for you. Shall I ask him to go into the hallway?"

They had decided that the groom would see the bride there and then the happy couple would step out together to where the guests were waiting. The ceremony would take place in the orchard, at the Williams family tree that had played a large part in Cade and Lily's love story.

Lily met April's gaze. "How do I look?" she asked with a nervous trill in her voice.

"Amazing," April assured her. "Cade will be speechless."

Lily wanted to leave the room, and her mother hurriedly pressed the bouquet in her hands. April kept the girls from following her. She was super curious what would go down in the hallway, once Lily was positioned there and Ma would fetch Cade. But such moments were personal, a thing between bride and groom. The rest of them would have the whole day to look at the happy couple and celebrate their joy with them.

She wondered for a moment how she would have felt, had she stood here without having won Matt's love. It would have been hard, she supposed.

She was glad things had turned out differently.

Ma came back in and said the two of them were together. She straightened the girls' headbands and then after having checked her watch a few times, said they could go out to meet the couple. Stacey and Ann ran ahead. April followed, with her mother and Gina in tow. Gina carried Barry on her arm. He was nine months now and a really bouncy cheerful baby who wanted to be a part of everything.

They found the happy couple hand in hand in the hallway. Cade looked like he was completely mesmerized by Lily in her bridal gown and she stared up at him with a smile as if she had never seen him before. April guessed that just a short while ago she might have rolled her eyes a little at this sight, but these days she understood completely. She couldn't wait to see Matt.

The front door was opened, and the happy couple stood on the doorstep a moment in between the two stained glass panels with apples worked into them. They stepped outside the very front door that Pa and Ma had walked through to get married. It was good to do it this way, to connect with the generations before them.

The gathered family, friends and locals cheered and threw flower petals at the couple. April followed, one hand on Stacey's shoulder to keep her from darting out, her eyes searching for Matt among the guests. She saw him standing to her left, in a dark suit, his hair brushed back. Belle beside him wore a light blue dress. She stood hand in hand with Bobby who looked very smart in a jacket and dark jeans. Everyone had dressed up for the day.

Matt smiled at her and his lips formed words. "Love you."

She smiled and mouthed back, "Love you too."

The crowd sang a song for the happy couple which Cade's best friend, Wayne, had composed. He also accompanied them on his guitar. The romantic music underlined the tender mood. Then they all went into the orchard. On this hot July day the green leaves sparkled in the sunshine and the developing apples peeked through the foliage. They fanned out to stand around the family tree with a good view of the couple who stood before Mr. Jenkins, who was officiating. Dad would have loved to be here and witness this. April felt a stab inside as she pictured him present at this ceremony, smiling at all of them. But then Matt came to stand beside her and caught her hand. The sadness felt less intrusive as she stood there, connected with both the past and the present, those who had passed away and those who were still among them. All united into one big family.

She felt so happy being here, being part of Cade's big day and having Matt by her side. Without looking at him she knew every detail of his face, every change in his expression as he watched these two tie the knot. She was so close with him and it was amazing. It hurt every time they had to say goodbye. Usually over the phone since she was still working and didn't have much leave. But Matt had known that and he was good with it, he said over and over. Still it couldn't go on for long. She had discussed with her boss that she was leaving at the end of the year. That was sooner than she had figured when Matt had come to her on the ship in Acapulco to confess his love for her, but then she hadn't known how much she'd miss him and how eager she was to start their life together. Her boss had been rather disappointed that she was quitting so soon after being promoted and asked her how they'd ever find someone as capable to take her place. She had mentioned a few people she considered especially able to move up the ranks and hoped that her decision to leave would prove to be an opportunity for one of them. She hadn't told Matt yet. She would find a quiet moment for that later today.

"I do," Cade said. His voice carried so much tenderness that April had goosebumps.

"I do," Lily said, beaming up at her groom as Ma wiped a tear away. Underneath the family tree where Pa had died of his heart attack. They had been forced to let him go at a time where they had felt they needed him most. But today April knew that her father's legacy was alive. No matter what obstacles life threw in their paths, the Williamses would always find their way back to each other. There was nothing here but happiness and gratitude and togetherness. They were family and they would always be.

Once the vows were spoken and the rings exchanged, the groom could kiss the bride. As Cade leaned down, everyone cheered and threw more flower petals. The photographer's camera clicked and clicked. Stacey and Ann came to stand with the couple for more photos. Then Ma, Gina and April joined Cade, and Lily's parents came to stand by her side. They were all smiling into the sunshine. There hadn't been such a big festive celebration on the ranch in many years.

While the guests chatted amongst each other, April helped carry out the refreshments to the large tables set up at the orchard's entrance. She helped Stacey get a glass with pink lemonade when Ma stood beside her. "There is one tray of cupcakes missing. Could you go and get it from the kitchen? I think it'll still be in the fridge."

They had put the cupcakes in the fridge to get cold so the frosting wouldn't immediately melt off in the warm day. April nodded and hurried away.

She went into the house that was very quiet after the bustle outside. In the kitchen she opened the fridge. There was a large silver platter with a silver cover inside. Was that it?

She pulled it toward her and lifted the cover for a peek underneath. There were no cupcakes. Indeed no other edibles. Just a postcard. It had four photos: of Matt's hotel ranch, the water mill, the church and the orchards in bloom and read, With Love From Heartmont.

Puzzled, she reached for it and turned it over. On the back it said, "Will you marry me?"

She stood and stared at it. Then she heard a sound behind her back. She turned around still holding the platter and the card. Matt stood and smiled at her. He looked amazing in his formal attire. More handsome than ever. And he had put the card here?

He was asking her...

Matt stepped closer and pulled the platter and the postcard from her hands. He put the items away and then took her hands in his. "April..." His voice caught for a moment. "I'm so glad you're here today and I am and...we know exactly how it is between us. It took us a long time to figure it out but then good things often take time. I never felt sorry that I waited so long for you, because you were worth waiting for. Now, I know this little town Heartmont is a simple place compared to all the cities you've been to and we don't have a lot to offer compared to the sights you've seen, but there's one thing Heartmont does have. Love. Lots of it. And I hope you want to live where love is. Do you want to marry me?"

April's heart filled with a rush of joy. It brimmed; it overflowed. Tears pushed behind her eyes and she said, "Yes, oh yes, Matt, I do."

He hugged her, held her close and she couldn't believe this was really happening to her. That he had asked her, even before she'd given up her career and…it was just perfect.

He loosened his grip a little and she looked up at him, saying, "You know how I feel about Heartmont, you, Belle… There is no place I'd rather be."

Matt grinned. "Good. Because there was no way I was going to let you go again. If you had said you wouldn't come and live with me here, I would have had to change professions and come work on the cruise ship with you."

April shook her head. "That's really not necessary. I've seen my share of the world. It was a wonderful time in my life. And we will always have all the postcards I sent to remind us of it. But this…" She held up his card. "Is the one postcard I want and need. The one I will always cherish."

Matt leaned down to her and brushed his lips over hers tenderly. "Believe me, this is only the beginning."

* * * * *